MENTAL PAUSE

ANNE LOUISE O'CONNELL

OC
Publishing

First published by Anne Louise O'Connell in 2013 and re-released in 2025

ISBN 978-0-984-9272-2-7

Cover design by Creationbooth – www.creationbooth.com

DISCLAIMER

None of the characters in this book exist in real life.

PRAISE FOR MENTAL PAUSE

"Deftly-drawn and enticing characters kept me entertained throughout this quirky romp through one woman's menopausal misadventures. Spiced with evocative descriptions of menopause's mental and physical onslaught, as well as spot-on dialogue and savvy passages that capture some of the complexities of female friendships, I read this great debut novel in a single sitting."

— AMSLIE, AMAZON REVIEWER

"I am sure it will speak to millions of women who can like me, identify with the message. In fact, more stories should be written about this since it touches so many. Also, the novel is fast paced, thriller-esque, and funny at times. I found it very different and inventive. Haven't come across a book that speaks about this, at least not in the fiction genre."

— ZVEZDANA RASHKOVICH, AUTHOR,
DUBAI WIVES

"I think this author may have created a new genre: meno-mystery! Who would ever think of combining menopause and murder? Your answer to that question probably depends on whether you have gone through menopause! Anne O'Connell does a great job of describing the physical and emotional turmoil that menopause causes. The fact that she manages to do this in a story that is both humorous and suspenseful makes this an enjoyable read."

— JAXON, AMAZON REVIEWER

This book is for all my friends and family who have been there before, especially my big sister Sue who has been there, done that, bought the t-shirt and then handed it off to me!

CHAPTER 1

Abbie opened the freezer, pulled out a loaf of bread and held it against her cheek. It was such a relief. She grabbed the eggs and milk from the fridge and began setting the table. She hadn't slept well and her head was pounding. It felt as if she was standing in the middle of a 21-gun salute. How long were these night sweats going to last? It seemed to be getting worse rather than better.

"Morning Mom." Her eldest son, Trevor shuffled into the kitchen and grabbed the glass of orange juice Abbie had poured. He downed it in one long swig. He was actually only four minutes older than his twin brother, Winston, yet Winston was the one who seemed to have wisdom beyond his 17 years. Both boys were very bright and usually lit up her days.

"Is your brother up yet? You'll have to get crackin' or you'll be late for school."

Trevor laughed and jerked his head to get what Abbie considered the way too long blonde bangs out of his eyes. He thought she was being funny. Abbie wasn't in the mood and just scowled at him, holding the spatula so tightly in her hand that the jagged edge of the handle that had broken off years ago, dug into her palm. "How many times do I have to tell you, I hate looking at you through that stringy hair...you need to get it cut before graduation. Now, go get your brother." Abbie waved the spatula in the direction of the kitchen door.

"Okay, chill . . . I'm going . . . morning Dad." Trevor squeezed by his father both of them turning sideways to get through the kitchen doorway at the same time. Both boys had their father's tall, broad-shouldered build. She caught him as he shrugged his shoulders at his dad and motioned his head in her direction. Conrad shrugged back. Abbie quickly turned and busied herself trying to open the bread bag so they wouldn't see that she had noticed the exchange. Someone had tied a knot in the top and it had frozen solid. She slammed it into the sink. "I guess I need some scissors," she mumbled under her breath.

"Morning babe. Whatcha doin'? Need some help?" He walked over and planted a kiss on the top of her head. She usually loved it when he did that... used to think it was sweet. This morning Abbie felt an unreasonable irritation burbling up.

"What does it look like I'm doing? I'm making breakfast," she snipped.

Conrad had been a beat cop for 15 years. He was desperately hoping for a promotion to detective. And, he constantly questioned everything, practicing for the day he would become an investigator. It used to be a fun game, like playing 20 questions and she and the boys always tried to stump him, but he usually guessed within 10. She wasn't in a playful mood.

"No, I mean with that?" He pointed to the Teflon pan sitting on the stove.

"I was going to scramble some eggs." Her thumb caressed the egg that was settled in the palm of her hand and she imagined bits of shell, yolk and egg white dripping down the side of his face. She clenched her teeth and with all the restraint she could muster, set it on the counter turned to face him and crossed her arms.

"Not with that you're not. Are you trying to kill us all?" Conrad shook his head and plunked onto the bar stool at the kitchen island and poured himself a cup of coffee. "Well?"

Abbie realized he was obviously waiting for an answer. She felt as if she was in the interrogation room at the police station.

"What in God's name are you talking about? And, I'd appreciate it if you wouldn't be so patronizing." She was desperately holding on to her last thread of patience and the cannons in her head were getting closer and going off more often. She rubbed her temples and tried to focus on what he was saying.

What she really wanted to say was that he was such an asshole. And, maybe she *was* trying to kill him. That would certainly get a reaction out of him. She wasn't a child. How dare he scold her like that! A hundred comebacks rolled around in her head but she just couldn't form the words. She didn't want to fight. They never usually did. They had always been able to resolve their differences calmly, without any name-calling or shouting. But lately, it didn't take much to make her want to jump down his throat. He really wasn't an asshole. He was actually a very sweet, kind and loving husband and father. He was a real anomaly in the law enforcement world. She had heard so many stories from the other wives about how the job had made their husbands cold and remote. Conrad seemed to be able to separate his work life and home life and was always in a good mood at home.

She looked at him leaning on the island that they had installed together and tried to bring back the memories of how much fun they had doing odd jobs around the house. They

3

were a real team. They had installed the island to make more counter space to enjoy their other favorite hobby. They loved to cook, which was a good thing since the whole family loved to eat too. Unfortunately, the recollection wasn't helping her mood any. *EVERYTHING . . . IRRITATES . . . ME!* Her mind screamed but she pursed her lips, grit her teeth and swallowed the bitter retort and just glared at Conrad waiting for him to reply.

"The Teflon in that pan is scratched and as soon as that seal breaks, poison starts seeping out of it. I've told you that before," he continued in his typical, matter-of-fact, non-accusing, yet somehow scolding manner.

Abbie just kept boring holes with her eyes, wanting to tell him to make his own damn breakfast. But she took a deep breath, counted to ten and, knowing he was right, turned the burner off, grabbed the pan and turned toward the back door. She took a few more deep, cleansing breaths, remembering her yoga teacher's instructions, unclenched her teeth and waited for her heart to stop pounding.

"Jeez. I'm so sorry. You're absolutely right. I meant to throw this out when I noticed the scratches last week. I'll do it now. Will you put on some toast, please, so the boys have at least something to eat before school?" It took all of her willpower to sound semi-normal. *I sound like a Stepford wife . . . he must think I've totally lost it.*

"Sure." Conrad picked up the loaf of bread out of the sink and effortlessly undid the knot. "Rough night, eh?" Abbie knew Conrad was trying. It seemed to her that he was struggling to understand.

"How the hell did you get that friggin' bag open so easily?" Abbie whispered under her breath. Conrad didn't hear her or chose to ignore her. He was probably wondering what was happening to his typically efficient and sweet wife, who took everything in stride and was usually the referee and cheerleader. Abbie wondered what had happened to her too.

"Yes, last night was rough. A real sauna," she agreed as she shuffled into her flip-flops sitting by the back door and felt another flush of heat starting in her bone marrow. She unbelted her robe and opened the back door, welcoming the cool morning breeze that wafted in around her and up through her night gown... the third one she had put on after changing twice through the night.

The breeze felt good but didn't eliminate the memory. There she was, lying flat on her back in bed with the bedclothes tossed to the side, trying not to let anything touch. Her skin so hot that it felt as if it was going to melt off the bones. The sweat hadn't started just yet but she knew it wasn't too far behind. Oh, there it was . . . the prickly feeling, followed by a pool of sweat forming in that little pocket at the base of the throat, just above the collarbone. The sun was coming up and Abbie could see the light through the crack in the black out curtains. Conrad slept at odd times of the day so they were special curtains that made the room dark enough to trick his body clock into thinking it might still be night and time to sleep. The cat was crying to go out and Conrad subconsciously reached over to stroke her arm . . . *ow!* It seared.

The night sweats. Abbie had been experiencing them every night for months. It's a slow boil that builds up to spontaneous combustion. It starts simmering in the bone marrow and then seeps into the blood stream. Then it comes to a boil and spreads through the whole circulatory system continuing until it emanates into the muscles and eventually breaks the barrier through to the skin's surface where it hovers for a moment as you're seared from the inside. The skin is momentarily dry and hot to the touch then bursts into droplets of salty, stingy, evil bands of sweat beads that roll en masse and group into pools. They sit in troughs under the eyes, camp out in crevices between and under the breasts, at the base of the throat and on the upper lip. The skin becomes slimy and slippery—the sweat demons then retreat, evaporating and leaving a tacky stickiness behind. Then the shivering starts.

Abbie had slipped quietly out of bed, reached into her cupboard and blindly pulled out a random t-shirt to put on to soak up the sweat and be a barrier to any touch. She went to the bathroom and looked in the mirror. *Oh my God . . . how ironic is that?* The t-shirt she was wearing said, "I'm out of estrogen and I have a hand gun . . . any more questions?" It had a yellow-eyed, glaring, scrawny, black cat on it. Maybe she would feel better if she had a shower. She took off the t-shirt she had just put on, pulled back the curtain and stepped into the tub. Abbie felt the relief as the tepid water rinsed the stickiness off. She toweled off, put her t-shirt back on and climbed quietly back into bed hoping she hadn't totally grossed out Conrad who, Abbie knew, was pretending to sleep soundly. She figured he just wasn't quite sure what to say. *Poor guy.* She really felt for him but couldn't quite bring herself to sympathize with his plight in understanding it, or her, when she was trying to deal with the shifting, swirling, swinging emotional and physical turmoil herself.

Abbie sighed. This was going to be a long summer. She stepped out onto the back porch and braced herself as she felt the telltale pinpricks. *Oh joy! This is the first time it's happened in the morning.* She crossed the back yard, carrying the poisonous pan in one hand and flapping her robe with the other trying to get some air circulating. She started to sweat profusely. Rivers flowed down every fold in her body, in some parts she hadn't realized had become crevices. She knew she must look pretty disheveled as she hadn't had a chance to comb the knots out of her hair after tossing and turning and sweating all friggin' night. She giggled to herself imagining her neighbor Bess's reaction if she happened to look out the window right at that very moment. Abbie was sure she looked like the wild woman from Borneo. The kids had to be at school so damn early so she was always up before six a.m. She hoped it was too early for Bess, or any of the other neighbors for that matter, to be up.

She opened the back gate onto the alleyway where they kept the garbage bins. *Oh shit! What a bloody mess.* Abbie looked in dismay at the remnants of the barbecued T-bones from the night before that were now strewn all over the back walkway. The bin lay on its side wobbling slightly to and fro in the breeze.

"Damn cats! This is all I need. How about a little break, hey?" She glanced up at the sky her free hand on her hips. A whimper caught in her throat, distracted for just a second, as she pinched the roll on her waist and thought about its ever-widening girth. She exhaled with an 'oh woe is me' moan and bent over to start collecting the debris as she wiped the sweat from her forehead with her forearm before it could drip into her eyes. She caught some movement out of the corner of her eye, and then heard a low, guttural, growl.

Abbie slowly turned toward the sound and there, about five feet away, snarling and growling was the mangy pit bull from down the street that had been terrorizing the neighborhood for years. His owner had been court-ordered to keep the thing muzzled and chained in the back yard after it had attacked and seriously injured a young child but it kept getting out. Abbie had called the police several times, to no avail. She had just commented to Conrad the day before that it was going to kill someone before anything would be done about it. He had shrugged it off saying that there were more pressing cases they were dealing with.

Abbie stood frozen to the spot as the guttural growls intensified. She could feel the rumbling vibration in the pit of her stomach. New sweat rivulets had sprung out and were pouring into her eyes and stinging. She couldn't see very well, not only because of the sweat dripping in her eyes, but she had also forgotten to put on her glasses. She could see he was getting closer though and the snarling was getting more menacing. She felt her arm starting to rise above her head in slow motion. It was as if it was under someone else's control. The frying pan in her hand had been forgotten as she was distracted by the sensation of every single pore in her body pulsing with heat and the shear panic rising in her throat.

He meant business. Abbie sure didn't want to be the next person he mauled. Suddenly, her panic turned to anger. *How dare he come into my back yard and threaten me?* Abbie's jaw clenched. She closed her eyes against the stinging sweat, tightened her grip... and followed through with an arcing swing like all her years of tennis lessons had taught her.

CHAPTER 2

Abbie walked slowly across the back yard not really grasping what had just happened and walked in the back door.

"Conrad? Trev?" She called as she came in the back door.

"Hey Mom... Trev's upstairs and Dad's gone to work," said Winston.

"Oh."

"What's wrong?"

"Uh...nothing. Well, I guess something." She wasn't sure what to say. *Your mother just creamed a dog on the side of the head with a frying pan and I think it's dead?* "Sweetie, can you call Animal Control for me? The number's in the book."

"Why?"

"Well, you know that awful, vicious white dog from down the street?"

"You mean the pit bull?"

"Uh huh. I think it's in our alleyway and I don't think it's alive.

"Oh wow... that sucks. Why can't you call?" Winston slathered a swath of peanut butter across his toast.

"I'm going to Rachel's to get ready for the marathon tomorrow. You know . . . for the fundraiser for breast cancer research? I'm already late. Thanks for doing that." Abbie quickly walked out of the kitchen hoping he wouldn't ask any more questions.

"But Mom," he called after her. "You don't run."

"I know that honey but I'm helping with registration... and so are you, remember?" She paused halfway up the stairs waiting for his reply.

"Oh right . . . shit, do I have to? Why isn't Trevor going?"

"Winston, that language isn't necessary and yes, you have to. You've made a promise to Rachel and it'll look great on your resume. And, Trevor's working. If you had gotten a job for the summer you'd have an excuse too."

"I'm still writing exams and I have to study!"

"Winston, you told me you didn't have an exam until Tuesday and you'd have Sunday and Monday to study. It'll only be for a couple of hours and it'll be great experience for you. Besides, Rachel's counting on you." Abbie turned and continued up the stairs hoping that was the end of the discussion. She could hear Winston mumbling and a couple of cupboard doors slamming but no further arguments followed. He had always liked Rachel and he more than likely wouldn't want to let her down.

Abbie quickly showered and changed into jeans and a t-shirt and grabbed her purse and keys.

"Trevor, I'm going to Rachel's but I'll have my cell phone on me if you need anything." She popped her head into his room and saw he was studying. Even though both boys had been accepted into university, it was conditional on their final marks. "When you come home from school, there's a pizza in the freezer for lunch if you want... or just make yourself a sandwich. And, you better hurry or you're going to be late.

You know it's always the last day that the teachers give the best clues on what's on the exam."

"Okay Mom. Say hi to Rachel for me."

Abbie walked down the stairs and straight for the front door, not wanting to make things worse with Winston, and called over her shoulder, "Winston, don't forget animal control. See you later!" She closed the door sharply behind her to make sure he knew she meant business. The boys knew she was a softy. It was Conrad who was the disciplinarian. Now that they were about to leave the nest, the relationship between them all was starting to shift. They were becoming adults and they finally realized that even though their father was tough, he was fair. Having a cop for a father wasn't easy but they had turned out pretty good. Abbie was very proud of her family... and loved them with all her heart. So, why was she so irritated by them now and why did she get angry so easily? She felt as if she was having out of body experiences and didn't recognize the person she looked down on half the time. It was as if she was having miniature nervous breakdowns and they were becoming more frequent.

She got into the car, mounted her cell phone on her hands-free, pressed '2' and 'send' and hit the speaker button. Conrad had the coveted number one spot on the speed dial but her best friend, Rachel, was next. She backed out of the driveway as Rachel answered.

"Hey chicka! Where are you?"

"Hey Rach. I'm sorry. I got a little behind but I'm on my way. I should be about 20 minutes as long as the traffic isn't too bad."

"No worries. Take your time. I'm just putting on a pot of coffee so it'll be ready when you get here. The kids are going to Todd's after school today for the weekend so we won't have any interruptions. Love those girls but they need to be entertained constantly! They can't seem to occupy themselves like your boys did at that age."

"Hmm . . ." Abbie offered absent-mindedly, not really hearing what Rachel was saying. "I might need something a little stronger than coffee though. You're not going to believe what just happened. I had a bit of a run in with a neighborhood dog."

"What?"

"I think I might have killed it." Abbie felt a lump rising in her throat. She tried choking it back but the sob escaped from her lips like an uncontrollable sneeze only with a mournful sound. She sniffed and gripped the steering wheel with one hand while she reached in her purse for a Kleenex.

"Oh my God honey! Are you okay?

"I don't know. I feel all hopped up, like I'm on speed or something. Things are just so out of control."

"What things?"

"Oh God, everything!"

"Jeez, are you sure you can drive? What dog? Are the boys okay? Is it Conrad? Do you want me to come and get you?"

Abbie took a deep breath. "No, no. It's nothing like that. Everyone's fine. It's me. I think I'm cracking up."

"Oh honey, I'm sure you're not. Just take a deep breath. Are you sure you can drive and don't need me to come get you?"

"No, I'll be okay. I'm halfway there now." Abbie snuffled.

"Then get yourself over here quick, but drive carefully... and we'll get it sorted out. We always do."

"You're right. I can always count on you. I'll see you soon."

ABBIE PULLED into Rachel's driveway, switched off the car and leaned her head on the steering wheel. Rachel was her best friend. They'd been through so much together... had seen the good the bad, the ugly and downright bizarre and still loved each other. She wouldn't think she was a beast for what she had done, would she? Could Abbie tell her what was going through her mind half the time? Would she think she was crazy?

Rachel knocked on the window and Abbie lifted her head, startled.

"Are you coming in or are we going to sit in the car?"

"No, no... I'm coming," Abbie smiled with relief to be in the company of the one person who knew all her deepest, darkest secrets. Not that she had that many but she and Rachel had gotten into some shenanigans way back when. They'd known each other since college and lived in the same dorm. Abbie was a resident assistant and a senior and Rachel was a freshman. They had been inseparable that year and even after Abbie graduated they were just a phone call away from each other.

If she could trust anyone with her innermost thoughts and feelings (no matter how crazy), it was Rachel.

They walked arm in arm into the house that Rachel had won in her divorce settlement and Abbie rested her head on Rachel's shoulder, feeling better already.

She plunked herself down on the familiar couch and grabbed her favorite puffy pillow and hugged it to her stomach. Rachel handed her a cup of coffee.

"You know I don't take milk. This one must be yours," Abbie went to hand the coffee mug back to Rachel.

"That's not milk sweetheart, it's a shot of Bailey's. 'Something stronger than coffee' you said. Sounded like you needed it."

Abbie looked at her friend and hesitated.

"Don't worry, I won't tell anyone. If it makes you feel better, I'll have one too. It'll help with our creativity." Rachel flashed the big, bright toothy grin that Abbie had always loved. "Now... spill it! Tell me what's going on."

Rachel plopped down on the couch and impatiently flicked the black curl that had bounced into her eye. She reached for the bottle of Bailey's on the antique trunk that doubled as a coffee table. She and Abbie had picked it up at a flea market for a steal. She poured a hefty dollop of the creamy liqueur into her coffee and sat back expectantly.

"Oh my Lord. I don't really know where to start."

"How about the dead dog. Were you joking?"

"Ummm . . . no, I wish I was."

Abbie took a long sip from her spiked coffee and sighed. Not only did it taste divine but she could also feel the soothing warmth of the liqueur coat her throat on its way down. It enveloped her stomach like a calming fuzzy blanket on a cold winter night.

"Do you remember the pit bull from down the street?"

"You mean the one who mauled that poor little kid and the court only ordered the owner to muzzle it and keep it chained in the back yard?"

"That's the one. Well, it met the business end of my frying pan in my back alleyway this morning."

"I'm sorry . . . what did you say?" Chuckling, Rachel slowly put her coffee down and put her hand gently on Abbie's knee. "Your frying pan?" Rachel was struggling to make sense of her friend's disjointed story.

"I'm pretty sure he's dead. I told Winston to call animal control and then left."

"Honey, you're going to have to back up and bring me into the loop," Rachel sympathetically offered, trying to help Abbie refocus. "Now, start at the beginning and tell me everything."

"I'm a terrible person," Abbie whispered, not knowing quite where to start.

"Oh Abbie, you are *so* not a terrible person. That dog should have been put down ages ago. Did it attack you?"

"I think he was about to so before I even knew what I was doing I took a swing at him."

"Well, you had no choice then. Um, you left out one thing. What were you doing in your back alley with a frying pan?"

Abbie took a deep, shuddering breath and swallowed hard to fight back the tears that threatened to start again. She looked pleadingly at her friend and hoped she wouldn't have her committed.

"Well, that sort of takes me to the next part of the story and why I'm losing it. I was throwing it in the garbage because Conrad said I was trying to poison everyone."

"O.K. Hold it right there. What do you mean, 'poison everyone'?"

"You know when Teflon gets scratched it emits some type of toxin?"

"No, I didn't know that. I'd better throw a few of mine out then too." Rachel squeezed her hand. "So, go on."

"I really meant to throw it out the last time I used it but I forgot and was going to fry eggs this morning and Conrad got kind of nasty... well, not really, but I was hyper-sensitive. I had a really bad night. You know, night sweats practically every hour and I couldn't sleep and had nightmares when I finally fell asleep and . . . God I'm a mess." Abbie dropped her face into her hands, shaking her head.

Rachel moved closer and wrapped her arms around Abbie.

"You're not a mess... you're just in mental pause." She gave Abbie a reassuring hug and chuckled again sympathetically. "I started about two years ago so I feel your pain."

"Two years? Really? But you're younger than me!" Abbie looked at Rachel suspiciously. "And, why don't I ever see you having hot flashes? Will it really last two years?"

"Actually, from what I've read it could be up to ten."

"Oh my God! Up to ten years? I don't think I can last that long."

"Sure you can. Women have been doing it since the beginning of time. You just find a way to manage it that's best for you."

Abbie hadn't realized Rachel was already there. She never complained.

"I feel so foolish. You're obviously stronger than I am."

"Not necessarily. Everyone experiences it a little differently. Tell me what makes you think you're losing it?"

Abbie thought about the first time her mind had gone off on a wild tangent and considered not sharing it. It was embarrassing and a little scary. But, she had to tell someone.

"Honestly Rach, if you could hear what's running through my head half the time you'd have me committed."

"Come on, it can't be that bad. When I first started I imagined a hundred different ways to kill Todd but then I just decided just to leave him instead." Abbie pulled away and stared in disbelief at her friend. "No! I certainly don't mean you should leave Conrad." Rachel continued hurriedly. "Todd and I were already on the rocks. You and Conrad are solid. But I'm just saying that it's normal to have some crazy thoughts when your hormones are raging."

"Okay . . . here goes," Abbie heaved a big sigh. "Remember a couple months ago when Conrad and I had a little escape weekend to Nantucket?"

"Yeah, I remember."

"Well, it was a particularly sunny, warm day, especially for April. Anyways, we rented a Harley and were cruising the island. I can't even remember what it was that set me off but I couldn't get my heart to slow down. My jaw was sore from clenching my teeth and all the sudden the thought occurred to me that all I would have to do would be to let go and lean backwards. We were on a highway with lots of cars coming from behind. It would be quick and I would be able to end the anxiety."

"Holy shit."

"I know." Abbie's eyes welled up but she felt a huge sense of relief finally sharing her thoughts with someone. "The only thing that stopped me was the realization of the mess that Conrad would have to clean up and how upset the boys would be and that they might blame their father."

"Wow, that's pretty extreme." As if on cue, Rachel's face became flushed as she broke out in an empathetic hot flash.

Abbie started to giggle and they both burst out laughing as Rachel grabbed a magazine from the table to fan herself.

"You know I've always been a really happy person. I've never, ever had suicidal thoughts. That's what scared me the most. And, these crazy thoughts just keep getting crazier. Maybe I've invented the mental hot flash."

Rachel shook her head. "Well, I'm sure there are others who have gone where no man has gone before. Sorry, I couldn't resist. I mean others who have had similar experiences. Any others you'd like to share?"

Abbie hesitated but then figured she'd taken her thumb out of the dam so she might as well tell all.

"Well, a few weeks ago we all went for a hike and the guys wanted to head up a hill that was off the trail. It was really steep and I thought it was too dangerous. We hadn't really prepared for anything too strenuous and I honestly wasn't up for it. They were adamant so I plunked myself down on a rock and told them to go ahead and I would wait right there."

"And?"

"They went ahead without me!"

"Well, you did tell them to."

"I know, and normally it wouldn't have phased me in the least. It was a lovely day. There were lots of birds to watch and I had my feet soaking in this perfect little stream. But then the irrational thoughts started. I imagined myself getting attacked and eaten by a bear." Abbie stopped and a giggle burbled out of her lips. She clamped her hand over her mouth as the giggle turned into a sob. Rachel scooted closer to her on the couch and put her arm around her shoulder.

"It's okay sweetie. You didn't get eaten, did you?" Rachel gave her a squeeze encouraging her to go on.

Abbie absentmindedly twirled a blond strand of hair between her fingers and a random thought occurred to her. "My roots probably need to be done, don't they? I know I look such a mess!"

"Abbie, your hair looks fine and you're not a mess," Rachel soothed and tightened her arm around her. "Now go on with your story."

"My brain just wouldn't slow down. I thought about them getting mugged and murdered because they had gone off the trail. And then I imagined them finding an exit somewhere on the other side and deciding that I was no fun anymore so they would just leave me behind and I could find my own way home... and, that they wouldn't really care if I did or not and they would probably be better off without me anyways!"

Rachel smiled. "You know Abbie, you've always been way too hard on yourself. I'm sure they love you even though you're a bit more irritable and moody lately."

"So, when this is all over, do I get me back? Will it be a new improved me or will I be a shell of my former self?"

"I guess we'll have to wait and see. But, if we don't get at these registration packets they'll never get done."

"You're absolutely right! Enough emotional ranting for one day."

"Honey, you can rant all you want, just start stuffing! I've got a friend coming by to help too. You're going to love her! She's a real riot and a half."

"Oh? Have I met her before?"

"No. She's in my 'newly single gal's' group. Her name's Joan and she's got quite a story too. But I'll let her tell you. I hear her pulling in the driveway now."

Abbie tucked her feet up under herself, sipped her coffee and closed her eyes. She loved hanging out in Rachel's living room. It had such a homey feel to it with its warm, pastel colors and nice big overstuffed couches and chairs and it always smelled like lavender. Rachel always had fresh flowers cut from her lovingly tended garden and liked to burn incense as well so it was like having aroma-therapy over coffee (or a glass of wine, depending on what time of day it was).

"Hey Joan, come on in. We're just having coffee in the living room. Can I pour you one?"

"Sure. Black, no sugar."

Abbie opened her eyes and almost dropped her mug. Joan was a stunner. One of those women who turns the heads of both sexes as she passes by, leaving jaws gaping.

"Hi I'm Joan." She dropped her purse on the chair by the door. "You must be Abbie! Rachel's told me so much about you. I feel we're already the best of friends."

Joan extended a long, graceful arm with a beautifully manicured hand, adorned with a gorgeous, and large, opal ring.

"Uh, hi . . . I'm Abbie . . . but you already know that," Abbie shook her hand, laughed nervously, and blushed. Or, was it a hot flash?

"I see you guys have introduced yourselves," Rachel handed Joan her coffee and held up the bottle of Bailey's. "We're having a bit of a decadent morning, want some?"

"Why not?" Rachel poured a generous splash into Joan's

mug and plunked down on the couch sandwiching Abbie in between them.

"Abbie's had a bit of a rough morning so we're helping her smooth away the rough edges," Rachel tossed her arm around Abbie's shoulders and gave her a squeeze.

"Well, cheers to cheering you up sweetie," Joan raised her mug in a toast.

"I'm feeling better now. We should really get to work with these registration packets or we'll never be ready by tomorrow."

They all got up and took positions along the assembly line Rachel had prepared and promptly fell into a comfortable rhythm of stacking and packing the cornucopia of literature, baseball hats, sunscreen and a litany of other sponsor give aways for the runners. Rachel, the epitome of event organization, had set up the materials methodically on tables and chairs in a circle around the living room so they were able to walk along and put one of each item in a bag and at the very end, winding up near the dining room where the completed bags were stacked on the table. Rachel and her husband had loved to entertain, so they had a humongous teak table with seating for 10.

The sound of a motorcycle starting startled Abbie and broke her bag-stuffing rhythm. Then the first bars of *Born to be Wild* followed.

"That's my phone," Joan said and reached for her purse, took her phone out and looked at the caller ID. "Shit, it's my husband. He calls at least five times a day." Joan stood up and started walking towards the front door. "Sorry gals, I have to take this. He still hasn't signed the divorce papers yet, so I'm trying to be nice."

"No problem . . . you go ahead and we'll keep stuffing." Rachel waved a ball cap at her. "I'll finish your bag for you so you don't forget where you left off."

Joan closed the door behind her. "That's gotta be tough," Abbie said getting back to the job at hand.

"Yeah, unfortunately, Joan's leaving took him by surprise and he's devastated. In denial, really."

"Hmmm . . . poor guy."

"She said she was surprised that he had no idea she was unhappy."

"Why was she so unhappy?"

"I think I'll let her fill you in when she's ready. We promise in the group not to share anything the others say with anyone else. I know I tell you everything but this is Joan's private stuff."

"Gosh, don't worry. I totally understand."

Joan came back in and re-joined the sorting and stuffing. She jammed a flyer into a bunch in the bottom of one of the bags.

"Everything okay?" Rachel asked and passed Joan her spiked coffee. "Those flyers sure are taking quite a beating."

"Fuckin' idiot," Joan hissed under her breath. "I just can't seem to get through to him, no matter how hard I try. Now he's begging me to go to marriage counseling."

"Aw hon, he's got to give up soon." Rachel put her hand on Joan's arm.

"I hope so. I reminded him that the best counselor in the world couldn't make our problem go away." Rachel nodded and gave her a hug.

"Jeez, what a bunch we are," Rachel laughed. "Crazy as a bag a hammers but at least we have each other, right?" They all raised their mugs in a toast.

Four hundred bags needed stuffing so they fell into a silent camaraderie. Abbie felt wrapped up in a cocoon of support and girl power with her companions. She wound up filling Joan in on the gory details of the morning and even found herself sharing more of the inner angst she'd been experiencing for more than a year. It felt as if she had been underwater in a murky pond and was bursting to the surface and taking a deep life-giving gulp of air after a never-ending free dive that had deprived her aching lungs of oxygen for so long. She couldn't help it... the words burst out of her like a stream overflowing in the spring thaw.

"I wake up exhausted every morning. I can't remember the last time I've slept through the night. My mind is hazy so it's hard to remember much of anything. I'm not sure what I put in these bags two minutes ago for heaven's sake! Last night it was three nightie changes and a pillow flip. I wish I could have changed the sheets but Conrad was sound asleep. I can't concentrate. I want to sleep in the middle of the day but there's always too much to do."

Rachel and Joan just kept listening, making sympathetic noises and nodding their heads.

Finally, after about the hundredth bag, Abbie took a breath and looked up from her bag stuffing.

"Jeez! I've been talking non-stop for two hours," Abbie glanced up at the clock on the wall. "I'm so sorry."

"You just needed to vent," Rachel offered. "What are friends for?"

"What you need is more girlie time sugar," Joan suggested. "You have two sons, right? Being surrounded by all that testosterone 24/7 can't be good for the constitution."

"I really love my boys and my husband but they are driving me crazy! I'm so tired of living in a frat house. Sometimes I think about taking a blowtorch to their rooms. But at the same time I'm scared to death to have them leave for college after the summer. What the hell will I do to keep myself occupied?"

"There's lots you can do but don't think about that right now. Let's get these finished and go get some retail therapy. I think it's time to get some sexy new outfits," Joan suggested.

"Then, after the run tomorrow, we're going to get our hair and nails done and I'm going to take you both out on the town tomorrow night!"

"Cripes! I haven't been 'out on the town' since the twins were born. I'll have to check with Conrad and see what the boys are up to," Abbie could feel a little glimmer of excitement swirling in the pit of her stomach but was also a little uncertain about the whole thing. "I really don't know if it's such a good idea."

"Don't be ridiculous! It'll do you a world of good. Just tell them you're staying the night with me," Rachel said.

"And going out on the town with two newly single divorcees. Conrad isn't going to like it." Abbie started clearing up the dirty coffee mugs.

Rachel rolled her eyes. "Not if you put it that way."

"Ah, and don't forget to tell him . . . one lesbian too," interjected Joan with a grin. "Now, let's go shopping!"

CHAPTER 3

When Conrad climbed into bed after his nightshift well after midnight Abbie was still wide-awake. The alarm was set for 6 a.m. and she had to be at the park to set up registration by 7 o'clock. The runners would begin checking in at eight and the run started at nine. She had to get some sleep but she couldn't stop thinking about Joan and their plans for after the run.

"How did the thing with Rachel go today?" Conrad yawned and leaned over to kiss her forehead.

Abbie leaned into his kiss, closed her eyes and sighed. "It went fine. We got a lot done. And, the 'thing' just happens to be a fundraiser for breast cancer research. I've told you a hundred times and you know how much this means to me. I wish you could be a little more supportive. It runs in my family you know."

"I'm sorry hon, long day. I know this is important and it's going to be great. You'll raise lots of money . . . " Conrad's voice trailed off and his breathing evened into the all-familiar sniff and wheeze.

At least he doesn't snore. Abbie thought to herself, rolled over and started counting sheep.

THE ALARM JOLTED her out of a very erotic dream. Joan had been in it and so had Rachel. There were limbs everywhere. She couldn't tell whose were whose but it didn't matter. Skin glistened, laughter peeled and hearts raced. Even awake, Abbie's heart was racing. She hoped she hadn't been talking (or moaning) in her sleep. What an insane dream. It was amazing how a little bit of information and a slight nudge can make the subconscious go wild.

Then she saw the shopping bag sitting on her dresser. She pictured the slinky little deep purple number inside that she had bought to wear 'out on the town' after Joan and Rachel assured her that it didn't show her muffin top. It had a swooping panel with pleats from hip to hip to camouflage the bulges that had formed almost overnight after she hit her mid-forties. It had a scooped neckline with a built in push up bra that the girls insisted made her boobs look perky. It had been a while since Abbie would have described them that way so she let her friends talk her into buying it, along with matching stilettos. She wasn't sure how she was going to walk in those but they did make her legs look great. Her legs were the one feature that Abbie still liked on her body.

After they had dropped Joan off when they were finished their shopping excursion, Rachel confirmed that yes, Joan was gay and had shared it with their singles group on day one. It was the reason her marriage had broken down. She had told the group that she had been suppressing it all her life. When she finally recognized why she always felt so out of place everywhere she went; why she felt stifled in her relationship; and finally left her husband, she blossomed.

Abbie was dying to know more and hoped there would be more stories shared in the day ahead. She tiptoed down the hallway to Winston's room, carefully sidestepping the creaky board after the third flower blossom on the runner and stopped in front of her son's door. The 'Keep Out... Dangerous Teenager' sign taped on the outside was left over from his early-teen years. It had actually been a gift from his brother who had bought one for each of them on their 13th birthday. Winston humored him by putting it up but had never been the typical unapproachable, uncommunicative teen.

She tapped lightly on the door and opened it a crack. He was still sound asleep. She opened it all the way and walked in and gently shook his shoulder.

"Come on sleepy head. Time to get going."

"Oh God... you can't be serious," Winston mumbled into his pillow.

"Yes, I sure am. I've already got some coffee in the 'to go' mugs and we'll pick up Egg McMuffins on the way."

That was his favorite breakfast so she hoped that would entice him. She'd found that, as with all growing teen boys, food was the all-time motivator for her crew.

It worked. "Okay, I'm up. Just give me 10 minutes to shower and throw on some clothes."

"Great. I'll be downstairs... and don't go back to sleep. I'm timing you! And, keep it quiet. Dad and Trevor are still asleep."

"No kidding," Winston whispered sarcastically as he shuffled down the hall toward the bathroom. Abbie shushed him as he tromped on the offending piece of wood she had so carefully avoided.

"Wait... you've got to wear the volunteer t-shirt and ball cap."

Winston turned and caught the package she tossed down the hallway to him.

"I hope they're not pink," Winston grumbled as he snatched them mid-air, still half asleep.

"Don't be difficult. They're black to differentiate us from the runners who will be wearing the pink ones. Now, hurry up!" She could feel the irritation rising as her pulse quickened and the pinpricks of heat started enveloping her, beginning at her knees. Some days the simplest of tasks seemed insurmountable, like getting Winston out of bed. *It had gone pretty smooth so why am I getting so anxious?* Abbie swallowed hard. And, there it was . . . the telltale lump forming in her throat. Her eyes started to fill with tears. She clenched her teeth. *What's wrong with me? This just shouldn't be such a big deal.*

She headed down the stairs and opened the front doorway to get a breeze just as the flush of heat coursed over her chin, spread across her jawline and rushed up to her scalp infusing every hair follicle with spiky sweat droplets. She sat on the doorstep fanning herself with the ball cap while she waited for it to pass. A sob escaped from her pursed lips and the tears marched down her cheeks joining forces with the sweat that had pooled under her eyes.

"God Mom, are you okay?" Winston came up from behind with both coffee cups in hand and sat down beside her. "I've only been 10 minutes."

"I know, I know. I'm just having a meltdown. I'll be fine in a minute." Abbie started breathing deeply. "Can you please go and get my clipboard and the car keys in the kitchen? And, just for today, can you please tie your shoelaces?" Abbie took another deep breath and wiped her cheeks. She shook her head as she looked at Winston's high top, unlaced sneakers.

"Sure." Winston shot her one of his *'Boy are you crazy'* looks, handed her one of the mugs and went inside.

Yes, I'm crazy, Abbie thought to herself. *I sure hope this doesn't get any worse. Feels like I'm bursting out of my own skin. Could be a scene from Men in Black.* Abbie took a few deep breaths and a gulp of her coffee. Where was the Bailey's? Surely that would be better than Prozac like her doctor had suggested.

"I'm already walking through so many days like a zombie," Abbie said absently into her mug and then blew on it to cool it down.

"What's that Mom?" Winston came up behind her and handed her the clipboard and car keys.

"Jesus, did I say that out loud?" She pulled her hair back into a ponytail and wrapped it in a pink scrunchy.

"Yeah . . . what'd you say?"

"Nothing. Let's get going or we're going to be late."

"Mom, it's Clasky Park right? It'll take us ten minutes max to get there. We're in plenty of time. You gotta chill."

Abbie glared at him and marched down the driveway. She slammed the car door, started the car and gunned the engine of her red VW bug.

"Mom, you know that's not good for this type of engine," Winston said as he got in beside her. "It's not a race car you know," Winston grinned and elbowed her gently. She knew he was just trying to tease her out of her mood. They all made fun of her little beetle bug but she'd always wanted one since the Herbie movies and she didn't care. They didn't have to drive it.

She jammed it in reverse and backed out of the driveway; took another deep breath; did her best to smile and turned on the stereo . . . loud. It was Joan Jett and the Black Hearts', *I love Rock 'n Roll*. Abbie started singing along.

Winston shook his head, rolled down his window and hung his elbow out and watched the sleepy neighborhood float by.

They arrived at the park in record time and the only others

that were already there were the rental guys setting up the tables, tents, chairs, port-o-potties, banners and the bouncy house and grills for the family BBQ at the end.

"See, I told you we'd be fine," Winston winked at her.

"Yes, you're right but you know I like to be early. That's us over there," Abbie pointed at the string of tables end to end at the entrance to the park with a huge banner over the top that read 'registration.' Just off to the right was the starting point of the run. The event management company was just adding the last of the pink and white helium balloons to the archway that all the runners would pass under at both the start and finish of the race.

Abbie wasn't running but she could feel the nervous excitement building in the pit of her stomach. It made her feel good to be doing something for the cause. Her mom had died of a very aggressive breast cancer after a short but difficult fight that included a double mastectomy and innumerable, grueling rounds of chemo. So far Abbie was clear, but she was diligent about self-examinations and having a mammogram every year.

"Come on love. Help me set up the chairs for the volunteers. Three behind each table. I'll get the sign-up sheets sorted out. Rachel should be here any minute with the goodie bags so you can help her unload those."

"Just give the orders and I will obey," Winston saluted.

Abbie swatted at him. He dodged and ducked and bounced around with his fists up. "Come on, put up your dukes."

Abbie laughed. "Come on, save that for later. Get to work!"

"Aye, Aye captain!" Winston saluted again.

He was such a good kid, Abbie smiled. Both her boys were. Good students, talented athletes and they rarely gave her an ounce of worry. Could be because they knew there would be hell to pay from their father, the cop, if they stepped out of line, but they didn't seem to mind. There was the occasional push back but nothing serious.

It was the perfect day for a marathon. Slightly overcast, temperatures in the mid 70s, a nice breeze coming from the nearby bay carrying her favorite summertime smell of lilacs in the air. The run was timed to be over before the mid-day heat and after that, Abbie was looking forward to the pampering Joan had planned for them. How nice it was to have Joan in her life to spice it up a bit. There was just something about her that made Abbie's knees wobble.

"Wow Mom, who's that with Rachel?" Winston interrupted Abbie's daydreaming. She looked towards the car park at the two women walking towards them, laden down with boxes and bags.

"Oh honey, that's Joan," she tried to sound nonchalant but her breath caught in her throat. Joan was wearing her volunteer shirt, just like Abbie's, but she had altered it. The sleeves were cut off into a tank style and she had it somehow knotted around her waist so her midriff showed.

"She's hot! This day could shape up better than I thought," chuckled Winston, his grin getting a little wider.

"Oh stop it. She's old enough to be your mother," whispered Abbie. "Well, don't just sit there. Go give them a hand!" Abbie smiled and waved at them and gave Winston a nudge towards them.

"Hey Rachel," Winston called. He ran up to them and gave her a hug and kiss on the cheek.

"Hey Win, it's great to see you. Thanks for the help today. We can definitely use a big strapping boy," Rachel and Joan giggled. "Winston, this is my friend Joan. Joan, this is Abbie's son, Winston."

"Nice to meet you Joan," Winston took the hand Joan reached out from under the box, stooped down and kissed it.

"Oh my, what a gentleman!" Joan curtsied flamboyantly.

"Don't be such a clown, Win. There's still tons of stuff in my car. Be a doll and get if for me will ya?" Rachel tossed him her car keys.

"Sure! Be right back," Winston jogged off to the parking lot.

"Hey Abbie! What a charmer your son is."

"I know. He's irresistible, just like me, right?" Abbie rolled her eyes.

"As a matter of fact, you're absolutely right," Joan leaned over the table where Abbie was standing and gave her a peck on the cheek.

Abbie grinned and leaned over to kiss Rachel's extended cheek too and gave her a big hug. "Thanks for yesterday. You're the best friend a girl could have."

"Don't mention it! You know I love ya babe."

Winston re-appeared with the remaining boxes and set them down next to Rachel and looked at her, awaiting his orders.

"Okay, Winston, just stack everything here on the table. Abbie, you start sorting the runners' t-shirts by size and Joan, all the goodie bags can go under the table at the far end. We won't need them until the runners start coming back. Just separate them by male and female – the guys' ones have the water proof money belt and the ladies' have the Gucci sunglasses." Rachel was in organizer mode and Abbie, Joan and Winston happily fell into the rhythm of following her lead along with the other registration volunteers who started arriving.

As Joan stashed her backpack under the table she nudged Abbie and winked at her. Abbie could see the cork of a wine bottle peeking out of the top.

"You're so bad!" Abbie whispered. "It's really too early and we've got to stay sober for Rachel... at least until registration's over."

Joan rolled her eyes. "Okay, I'll behave for now but it'll be there when we've been released from duty." She gave Abbie's waist a little squeeze with both hands as she shimmied behind her in the tight quarters of the booth and her breasts brushed across Abbie's back. Abbie dropped the sunglasses that were in her hand. Her heart thumped oddly in her chest as she scurried to pick them up and busied herself re-arranging the same bags over again.

"Hey, did you notice that guy across the street leaning against his car?" Winston squinted and put his hand over his eyes to shade them from the sun. "He's been snapping pictures."

"No, I didn't," Abbie's breath was coming in short spurts as she tried to concentrate on sorting through the paper squares with bold black numbers and safety pins that the runners would fasten to their shirts.

"Mom . . . it looks like he's taking pictures of us. Weird . . . he looks kind of like Columbo."

The boys had a thing for cop shows and had bought all the old TV series from *Columbo* to *Hill Street Blues* on DVD. It was quite likely that they would follow in their father's footsteps and pursue some type of career in law enforcement. Winston had talked about forensic medicine but said he was 'keeping his options open'.

"There's going to be plenty of press covering the run so he's probably a newspaper photographer."

"I guess so. I think he looks shifty."

"And, you've got an active imagination," Abbie replied. "Now stop gabbing and get to work."

Winston shrugged and turned to his assigned task.

All four hundred runners were signed in and at the starting gate in record time and the run went without a hitch. Rachel's team was ready and in position when the first runner came across the finish line. After the last goodie bag was handed out and the last thank you speech was given, the three ladies and Winston shared a round of high fives, slumped back in their chairs and propped their feet up on the table.

"Well girls, I have hair appointments and pedicures scheduled for all of us at Randy's Salon at 1:30 pm. Sorry Winston, you're not invited," Joan pouted at him, ruffled his hair and handed the bottle of wine to Abbie.

Rachel and Abbie went into peals of laughter. "He'd look pretty cute with pink toes," Rachel said, which set them all off into more fits of giggles.

"You guys are nuts. You sound just like the 10th grade girls at my school," Winston stood up and self-consciously smoothed down his hair. "Look, no worries, I've got to hit the books anyways. Mom, can you take me home?"

"Why don't you just take my car? I'll go with Rach and Joan and meet you back home later," Abbie tossed him her keys.

"Really? You never let me drive your car."

"Just this once and straight home, okay? And, be careful!"

"I will. See you guys later."

"See you Win . . . and, thanks for all your help. You're such a trooper," called Rachel after him. "Tell Trevor I said hello!"

As Winston escaped, Abbie linked arms with Rachel and Joan and still giggling like schoolgirls, they practically skipped to the car, eagerly anticipating their afternoon of pampering.

CHAPTER 4

The chairs were like the biggest, most comfortable lazy boys you've ever seen in your life. Abbie sat in the middle one, with Rachel and Joan on either side, eyes closed, feet soaking luxuriously in a warm, bubbly foot-bath attached to each chair. The chairs had built-in roller massagers that could be adjusted to whatever pressure and speed your heart desired. Abbie had hers set on slow and steady. It rolled from the base of her spine, over her butt cheeks, and made its delicious way, pulsating along the muscles that flanked her spine up to her neck and shoulders, pausing on the base of her skull, where it vibrated gently, and then started its happy journey back down.

Abbie squeezed the hands of her two best friends . . . one she had known forever and one who had just entered her life, just at the right time. She hadn't had a second of irritation, or one irrational thought for at least a couple of hours. She wished she could bottle this feeling and take it out whenever she needed it.

Joan squeezed back. "You know, if the rest of your family is anything like Winston, you're a very lucky lady."

"They are," Rachel replied for her. "Both boys are charmers and Conrad is as solid as the rock of Gibraltar."

"Yes, I guess I am . . ." Abbie didn't want to talk about her family. She wanted to pretend the only person she was responsible for was herself... just for a few hours. She felt the irritation rising and swallowed it back.

"This feels heavenly," she changed the subject. "I can't remember the last time I had a pedicure."

"Hmmm . . . I started having them regularly after my husband and I split up," said Joan. "I figured if I was going to be out on the singles scene again I'd better get fit. And, have pretty toes. You know, the important stuff . . . like smooth legs because you never know when you're going to be rubbing them up and down someone else's!" Joan ran her tongue along her upper lip. Rachel laughed.

"Right! I started doing a little regular pampering after I met Joan in our singles group," she added, smoothing down her newly highlighted hair. "She made me realize that if I was going to survive as a single mother I had to find a way to relax once in a while. It's actually easier now that Todd has the kids every other weekend and next week they'll be with him for the summer. I'll be a free woman!"

"You make it sound almost appealing," said Abbie wistfully.

"Actually, I miss them like crazy but I've gotta make the best of it."

"Do you mind me asking, how long have you been separated, Joan?" Abbie swished her feet in the foot-bath as the three technicians took their places on the stools at their feet.

"No I don't mind at all. As you heard from my phone call yesterday from my 'husband', he's dragging his feet on the divorce but we've been separated almost six months now." Joan shook her head and let out an exasperated sigh. "His lack of cooperation has made it really difficult for both of us. I guess I can understand. It was shocking for him when I finally came out of the closet, and it's really sent him for a loop." Joan picked out a deep red nail color from the tray of polish the nail tech held out towards her.

"On the surface, we were the perfect couple. Everyone thought so. I thought so too, to a certain extent, but there was always something that didn't feel quite right. The sex was okay but I rarely had an orgasm. It would only happen when I did it myself."

Abbie's eyebrows shot up and she squirmed a little in her seat.

"Oh, sorry about that. Am I making you uncomfortable?"

"Not at all . . . You listened to my troubles all afternoon yesterday. It's okay. Go ahead."

"Rachel knows the whole sordid story. I've bored her and our group with all the details before."

The pedicure girls were stealing sideways glances at each other, pretending they weren't listening, busily clipping and filing and buffing feet. But they were obviously hanging on every word.

"I'm never bored with you daaaa-hling, that's for sure," Rachel laughed. "We even compare notes on the different middle-aged, divorced women's singles' scenes . . . the gay and the heterosexual. There are more similarities than differences really."

"I'm so out of touch," Abbie lamented.

"Don't worry, we'll be gentle," Joan stroked her hand.

"Now, don't you be corrupting my best friend," Rachel warned. "I'll be the one who will have to answer to her husband."

"Very funny Rach. Don't you worry about me, I can handle Conrad," Abbie said defiantly as she felt the familiar rush of heat coming to the surface of her skin and the sweat pooling under her eyes and dripping down her temples.

"Abbie you're beet red . . . are you okay?" Joan leaned over.

"Yeah, you're witnessing the text book hot flash. It'll pass in a minute." Abbie fanned herself.

"So, that's what I have to look forward to... doesn't look like much fun to me," Joan twirled a strand of her long, wavy, dark hair between her thumb and forefinger. "You gonna be alright?"

"I'll be fine, but you know guys, you're going to think I'm a real wuss but can we do our big night out next weekend? It's been a really long day and I'd like to enjoy myself. When I drink in the middle of the day I just want to take a nap and that little bit of wine after the run really went to my head. At this point, I feel like I'd be dragging my butt."

"Of course. I guess we're going to have to ease her in Joan," Rachel patted Abbie on the hand. "Next weekend works for me. Or, any weekend after that for the rest of the summer," Rachel double hand-pumped the air.

Abbie and Joan laughed and leaned back to enjoy the rest of their pedicures.

"Okay, but I insist that when we're done we go grab a quick glass of wine at this awesome little wine bar down the street. We can't let these new hairdos completely go to waste," insisted Joan.

"You're incorrigible!" Rachel smiled and looked beseechingly at Abbie.

"You're damn right I am! How about it Abs?"

"Well okay. I think I can make it through just one."

They finished up at *Randy's* and as Joan promised, the wine bar was just a few blocks away. The girls practically floated their way there, totally relaxed from their pampering session.

"I swear Joan, over the last six months, you must have scoped out every little bar and lounge in town," Rachel held the door open.

"Oh, probably longer than that. I kind of started experimenting before I finally decided to leave my husband."

"Well, you're just full of surprises, aren't you?"

"Makes life interesting," Joan picked a spot at the end of the bar where the corner rounded.

"Hey Joanie, who're your friends?"

"Hi Jack. This is Rachel and Abbie. Girls, this is Jack, the best sommelier in town."

"You would know," replied Jack as he shook Rachel and Abbie's hands. "You've explored all the wine bars from here to New Hampshire."

"Now, ain't that a fact! But this one's by far my favorite. What's new this week?"

Jack got busy pulling bottles from the racks, explaining the different 'noses' and 'finishes'.

"Oh, I'm not staying long enough to try all those," Abbie put her hand up. "I'll just have a glass of your house cabernet, please."

"That's fine love. I'll give you a rain check any time." Jack put the bottles back. "And, for you lovely ladies?"

"Make that two," Rachel said.

"Alright you party poopers," Joan said. "I guess just a glass of Pinot Grigio for me, Jack."

CHAPTER 5

They had tried to convince her to stay out past one glass but Abbie stuck to her guns. She insisted they drop her home so she could check on the boys. Conrad was working until eleven and, even though she knew the boys would be studying, she had convinced herself that they still might need her.

It was just after six o'clock when Abbie came through the back door and into the kitchen, purposely not looking towards the back gate. It seemed like ages ago she had had the run-in with the dog. Winston had called animal control and they had told him they may need to contact her to get some details but would need to inform the owner first and get back to her. She hadn't heard anything so hoped the issue would be dropped since the dog had a record, so to speak.

"Hi boys, I'm home," Abbie called up the stairs. She stopped at Trevor's door and knocked.

"Come in."

Abbie opened the door and poked her head in. Both boys were bent over textbooks and laptops taking notes. "How's the studying coming along? Can I help?"

"Uh no... it's physics," answered Trevor. "How was the run? Winston says you have a new hot friend," Trevor grinned at her and Winston threw his pen at his brother. Trevor caught it and tossed it back.

"Don't you worry about my friend. You need to keep your mind on the books. Can I make you dinner?"

"Nah, we were hungry earlier and walked to McDonald's so we're good," Trevor motioned towards the crumpled brown bags on the floor and turned back to his book. She was dismissed. She wasn't needed.

"You guys eat far too much junk food," Abbie started to lecture and stopped herself. What was the use? She hadn't been there; they were hungry; they took care of themselves; end of story. Most mothers would be thrilled since other teenagers would be demanding 'what's for supper, I'm hungry' or looking for money. Abbie and Conrad had been giving the boys a weekly allowance since they were small and, other than the necessities, they knew if they wanted more, they had to do extra chores. They'd both had part-time jobs through their junior and senior years and would be working full-time this summer so they rarely, if ever, asked for money.

She turned around and closed the door quietly behind her as she felt the tears welling up in her eyes. You give your heart and soul for seventeen years for what? For them to leave you. Abbie knew she should be happy for them. They had both gotten into good schools on scholarships. Winston was going to Penn State and Trevor would be a little closer to home at the University of Massachusetts. It was still two hours away so he would have to live on campus. She was so proud of them but it wasn't fair, was it? What was she going to do? No one needed her anymore. They hadn't even noticed her new haircut. Of course they hadn't noticed five years ago when she started dying her hair blonde either. Conrad had made a passing comment about being married to a 'new woman' but hadn't really made a big deal of it. *Men!*

She shuffled into the kitchen, opened the freezer, grabbed a hot pocket and tossed it in the microwave then grabbed a beer from the fridge. *Real healthy Abbie.* She scolded herself. *The hell with it.* She threw in a second one and took a couple of swigs of beer while she waited for her supper to heat. She put her feast on a plate and padded into the living room, curled up on the couch and switched on the TV while tears coursed down her cheeks.

I'm definitely losing it. I've had a great day with two amazing friends, helped raise boatloads of money for a charity I feel very passionate about, had an afternoon of pampering, yet I'm blubbering like an idiot. She couldn't find anything worth watching and couldn't seem to shake her malaise. So, she downed the rest of her beer, stretched out on the couch, pulled up the patchwork quilt her mom had made her from all her favorite t-shirts she had collected over the years, and fell into a deep sleep.

IT WAS SHORTLY after one o'clock in the morning when Conrad came in from work. He gently shook Abbie's shoulder to wake her and she slowly opened her eyes and sat up.

He sat down beside her on the couch. "Who's drinking the beer?"

"Uh, I am . . . it's no big deal," Abbie said defensively, her hackles immediately raising.

"I didn't say it was a big deal. It's just you never drink beer. How was your day?"

"It was fine," Abbie said almost in a whisper and took another swig.

"Doesn't sound fine. What's up?"

"I don't know. I just feel so on edge all the time and I can't stop crying at every little thing. The boys had taken care of themselves for dinner tonight and I couldn't help thinking they don't need me anymore."

"Don't be so silly. Of course they need you. *We* need you. Maybe your hormones are just a little out of whack. Didn't your doctor suggest you try some type of hormone replacement thingy?"

Abbie felt her adrenalin spike, shocking her still sleepy head. She pushed him away and jumped up from the couch. "See, that's part of the trouble," she shrieked. "Just because you've arrived at the solution doesn't mean it's the right thing for me!" She heard her voice becoming hysterical but couldn't stop. "I don't want to take pills. I just want this to go away," she felt the anxiety rising in her throat and sent Conrad a scathing look.

Stunned, Conrad said nothing as she spun around and stomped up the stairs to their bedroom, slamming the door. She threw herself on the bed and sobbed uncontrollably.

He followed her into the bedroom and tried to take her in his arms. "GO AWAY!" She was inconsolable.

Conrad left the bedroom and she could hear muffled voices in the hallway. Suddenly it dawned on her that the boys probably heard it all. They probably thought she was nuts. She pushed her face into her pillow to muffle the sound and cried herself out.

When Conrad came back into the room a half hour later, Abbie was quietly sitting up; hugging her pillow staring at the small TV they had put in the bedroom so she could watch her shows while the guys watched sports. She usually loved to watch sports too but every once in a while she needed to balance it out with a chick flick or a helping of Oprah.

He sat next to her and pulled her into his arms.

"I'm sorry I've been such a lunatic lately."

"But you're my lunatic," Conrad kissed her on the forehead.

Abbie melted into his arms, closed her eyes and sighed deeply. She hoped he would be patient with her while she sorted through this phase. What did her mother always say? 'That which doesn't kill you makes you stronger.' She wasn't sure that this *wasn't* going to kill her.

Abbie drifted off to sleep cocooned in Conrad's arms.

CHAPTER 6

After yet another restless night, Abbie practically had to feel her way to the kitchen. Bleary-eyed she put on a pot of coffee and pulled out a box of waffles from the freezer. She left the door open and stuck her head in to cool off as the remnants of her last hot flash lingered.

"Anything good in there," Conrad patted Abbie's bum as he walked by.

"Just cooling down," Abbie replied removing her head from the freezer.

She poured herself a glass of water and popped a couple of Tylenol into her mouth.

Both boys had already left to play golf with some friends. She was glad she didn't have to face them this morning and try to explain her wild ranting and raving. They were teenagers. They'd have forgotten it already and be focusing on their golf swing and planning the party for grad night.

"Sorry about the drama last night," Abbie slouched onto a bar stool at the kitchen counter.

"Don't worry about it. I've dealt with tougher thugs than you," Conrad joked as he poured his coffee.

Abbie could feel a nasty retort building just as the phone rang.

"I'll get it," relieved, she snatched up on the second ring. "Hey Joan... no, you didn't wake us up... the boys are actually up and out already... lunch? Sure... I have no plans," Abbie covered the mouth piece and mouthed to Conrad, "We don't have plans today do we?"

"No, I'm headed down to the station so you go ahead," Conrad poured his coffee into a thermal 'to go' cup.

"Yeah Joan, that would be great," Abbie turned back to her phone conversation. "Where do you want to meet?... Okay, see you there at noon."

Abbie hung up the phone and leaped off the stool, welcoming the distraction.

"See you later then," Conrad called.

"Bye . . . " Abbie was already halfway up the stairs throwing off her bathrobe and jumping into the shower before the back door closed behind him.

ABBIE PARKED her little VW bug right in front of the restaurant where she was meeting Joan. She loved that she could squeeze into the littlest spots that the moms driving the gargantuan SUVs couldn't, leaving them circling waiting for a spot to open up at school pick up time.

Joan smiled and waved from her window seat as Abbie fed coins into her meter. Abbie waved back, slung her bag over her shoulder and breezed into the restaurant.

"Great spot!" Abbie said as she kissed Joan on both cheeks.

Joan had picked a quaint little bistro that Abbie hadn't been to before. It was brightly lit and had beautiful original watercolors on every wall depicting scenes of Paris and the

French countryside. There were potted plants, red, yellow and violet bursts of flowers in vases and ivy climbing up and around a wrought iron archway that led into the main dining area.

"Best view in the place," Joan agreed.

"Is Rachel coming?" Abbie looked around.

"No, it's just us. I think she had something to do with her girls."

"Oh right. I guess she's probably picking them up at Todd's right about now," Abbie looked at her watch. "This is her last week with them before they go to their dad's for the summer."

"Oh yeah... I guess that's right," Joan flashed a dazzling smile that made Abbie blush. "I picked a table right under the A/C. Looks like you may need it already," Joan teased.

"Ha ha," Abbie fanned herself but was very appreciative of Joan's sensitivity and sense of humor with her plight.

"So, how are things?"

"Not too bad. So glad you called though. There's way too much testosterone swirling around in my house."

"Happy to add some estrogen to the mix," Joan poured Abbie a glass of sparkling wine from a bottle already sitting on the table.

"Isn't it a little early for that?" Abbie laughed.

"It's Sunday brunch . . . we'll add a little OJ to it and that'll be your vitamin C." Joan shrugged. "Abbie, you've got to learn to live a little."

"You're absolutely right," Abbie raised her glass in a toast. *She was right, wasn't she? I deserve to have some fun . . . so why do I feel so guilty?*

"So, what do you carry in that huge mommy purse anyways?" Joan motioned towards the sack sitting on the bench next to Abbie.

"Anything and everything," Abbie laughed. "When you're

a mom, you've got to be ready for any disaster that might come your way."

"Let's see," Joan leaned over.

Abbie plunked the heavy burden on the table and started rifling through it. "Keys, wallet, handy wipes, lip balm, a granola bar, Kleenex, band aides, Trevor's old retainer. Good God, what's that thing doing in there?"

"Abbie, I think it's time you shed your 'mommy persona' and figure out who you are in here," Joan put her hand over her heart. "Those boys are all grown up."

Abbie could feel the tears prick behind her eyes.

"You know it's inevitable. They don't stay babies forever," she reached into Abbie's purse and grabbed a Kleenex and handed it to her. "Here's a question for you... when was the last time you did something without checking with your husband first?"

"I don't really remember."

"And, is there anything you've always wanted to do but knew he wouldn't be pleased so you stopped yourself from doing it?"

"Like what?"

"I don't know . . . hmmm . . . maybe shaved your head or pierced your nose."

"Eww, I wouldn't want to do either. But, I did dye my hair last year."

"Didn't he want you to?"

"He didn't really care. Didn't even notice to be honest."

"Okay . . . that doesn't count then. You have to think of something else."

"Well . . ." Abbie paused.

"Go on. I promise, I won't tell," Joan leaned in conspiratorially.

Abbie giggled. She was already feeling a buzz from the wine as she'd only had a cup of coffee so far and nothing to eat.

And, she was starting to feel the telltale pinpricks starting under her skin but ignored it. "I've always wanted to get a tattoo. Conrad hates them because he says they're for thugs and gang members. He sees a lot of those in his line of work."

Joan smiled and nodded. "I forgot he's a cop. But, I've seen lots of cops with tattoos."

"Not this one," Abbie took another sip. "He says your body is your temple and it needs to be treated with the utmost respect."

"Ah, but the most important fact is that it *is your* body and you should be able to decide what to do with it. And, besides, have you been to any temples lately? They've got lots of decorations and designs all over the walls."

"True. Well, we better order. I don't want to drink any more on an empty stomach." Abbie didn't open the menu right away, but fanned herself with it instead.

Joan rolled her eyes. "There you go, sounding like a mother again."

"I know," Abbie sighed. "But it's a hard habit to break. Once a mother, always a mother."

"Are you okay?" Joan sat back and fixed Abbie with a concerned look.

"Sure, why?" Abbie brushed the tiny beads of sweat that had broken out on her upper lip like mini-bubble wrap.

"Well, you're beet red and you're pouring down with sweat. Do you have a fever?"

"Ha, I wish!" Abbie dug in her purse and pulled out an individually wrapped wet wipe. "It's a damn hot flash," she said ripping open the package and mopping the rivulets off her face.

"Jesus, I keep forgetting. You look so young to be going through that shit already."

"Uh-huh." Abbie was already scanning the menu.

"You know, my sister's been battling this for a long time now and she finally found something that works for her."

"Oh yeah?" Abbie looked up.

"It's like hormone replacement."

"For Christ's sake Joan! Not you too. Everyone seems to be pushing pills on me. I don't like pills," Abbie voice raised an octave.

"Okay, calm down," Joan put her hand over Abbie's. "Just let me finish and then we can forget about it and never talk about it again, alright?"

"Fine. Finish what you were saying and then we'll drop it." Abbie sat back with her arms crossed, pissed off that Joan had gone and ruined her buzz.

"Come on, don't be like that. I'm only trying to help," Joan reached for the bottle and re-filled Abbie's wine. "There, that'll make you feel better." Abbie uncoiled and Joan continued. "All I wanted to say was that my sister found something called bioidenticals. I have no idea how they work, only that they're supposedly natural and exactly match your own so there are supposed to be fewer side effects."

Abbie took a sip of her wine and smiled. "I know you're just trying to be helpful and I'm sorry I bit your head off. I promise I'll look into the bio-whatevers, but for now let's order. I'm starved!"

They spent a companionable couple of hours, sharing intimate details of their lives over eggs Benedict and another bottle of sparkling wine. Abbie found her so easy to talk to and Joan took to the role of coaching Abbie on how to 'live a little' and 'be her own woman' with gusto. She'd been a wife and mother for so long she had forgotten what it was like to just be Abbie. She could be all three, couldn't she? Especially since the boys didn't really need her anymore. She kind of liked the idea of breaking free, just for a little bit.

"I have an idea," Joan said as she signed the check. Abbie tried to contribute but Joan insisted it was her treat.

"What's that?"

"I think we should go and get you a tattoo."

"Oh Joan, I don't think that's such a great idea," Abbie was digging in her big bag for her car keys. A tattoo was a little too 'free and easy' but she paused to let Joan's suggestion sink in. Why was she letting this woman dictate to her? Wasn't she just trading one dictator for another? *Get a grip Abbie... Conrad's not a dictator and neither is Joan. You've always wanted a tattoo so why not? Conrad will just have to love you the same with a little extra ink under your skin.*

"Don't be silly. It's a great idea. And, forget about your car. After a couple bottles of wine we really should take a cab."

"I don't know Joan, I should be getting home."

"For what? You said Conrad was working and the boys were going to be gone all day. Abbie, you deserve to do something just for you. To hell with them!"

"You know, you're right. To hell with them. It's my body and I'm going to get a tattoo!" Abbie stomped her foot. "Is there even a tattoo parlor in New Bedford though? I don't think I've ever seen one."

"Sure there is, but it's in an area of town you probably don't get to visit very often." Joan laughed and linked her arm through Abbie's and they walked side-by-side out of the restaurant. Abbie glanced down and for the first time, noticed a little tattoo on Joan's ankle... it was a pair of angel wings.

Joan hailed a cab and gave the driver an address. It didn't occur to Abbie to ask how she just happened to know the address of a tattoo parlor off the top of her head. She was just 'going with the flow' like Joan said.

The tree-lined city streets gave way to open space which turned into an industrial park which turned into a seedy side of town that, in truth, Abbie had never been before.

"You sure this is safe?" Abbie asked Joan as her eyes darted from one side of the street to the other, her previous bravado fading. This looked like the sort of place that Conrad might be called to a crime scene. Probably not somewhere she should be flippantly trouncing into with a veritable stranger without a second thought.

"Sure, there's an after-hours club here that I go to all the time. Don't worry." Joan paid the driver and grabbed Abbie's hand and coaxed her out of the car.

They walked into the tattoo parlor that actually looked a bit like a barbershop. It had the same type of chairs and there were even a couple of people reclining comfortably while the tattoo artists were jabbing ink-filled needles rapidly in and out of their arms. It looked like they were having matching tattoos done—a heart with an arrow through it and each other's names inscribed across the bottom (at least that's what Abbie assumed).

"Hi there, how's it going?" Joan walked to the counter and started flipping through the catalogue of designs. "My friend here would like to get a tattoo."

Abbie felt like a real rebel. She was scared but a little excited too. She and her mom had always joked about going to Key West together to celebrate Abbie's 50th and her mom's 80th birthdays (their birthdays were in the same month and they had always celebrated together on the day that was exactly in between). But her mom had died before they could call each other on their bluff. As an only child, Abbie and her mother were extremely close and the memory of her passing still triggered a sharp pain in Abbie's heart and a gnawing emptiness in her stomach.

Thinking about how much she missed her mom Abbie absentmindedly started to flip through the catalogue Joan had passed to her. "It can't be anything too big," Abbie began. "I want it to be understated. She stopped at a whole page of tattoos with the word 'mom' in them. *How appropriate would that be? If I did it in memory of my mother, how could Conrad get mad?* Besides... she was still a mom too but she'd be a wild mom with a tatt!

Abbie pointed to one that was a pink rose with the word 'Mom' written in a beautiful scroll across an open petal. "That's the one," Abbie pointed to it. "How much?"

"That's three hundred dollars."

"That's a great deal Abbie . . . go for it." Joan pushed her towards an empty barber chair.

"Okay, okay! Stop pushing." Abbie couldn't believe she was actually going to do it. "I have to pee first."

"I'll get the inks ready," said the man from behind the counter. Abbie assumed his name was Mike since the name was tattooed on his right bicep.

"Thanks Mike."

"Oh, I'm not Mike. That's Mike," he pointed to one of the other artists who was hard at work. "I'm Bill." Bill and Joan grinned at each other.

"O-okay, Bill," Abbie stammered. "I'll be right back."

Two hours later, as the taxi pulled up in front of the bistro where they had left their cars, Abbie marveled at how easy getting the tattoo had been. Sure her neck was a little tender, she had decided to get it behind her right ear, but after the first few minutes it had gone pretty numb.

"How does it feel?" Joan handed the driver two twenties. "Keep the change," she said as she slung her purse over her shoulder and opened the door.

"It's throbbing a bit but it'll be okay," Abbie admitted. They both walked around and met at the back of the taxi, next to Abbie's car.

"Yeah, it's probably going to throb for a while and then as it heals it'll get itchy," Joan caressed the sensitive skin on Abbie's neck around the tattoo. Abbie closed her eyes and leaned into Joan's hand. It was soft and warm and was pulsing with a comforting energy.

"Hmmm . . . that feels nice," Abbie murmured. "The throbbing's even going away."

"I'm so glad," Joan almost purred.

Abbie opened her eyes and slowly pulled back. "Y-you have um, healing hands," she stammered. "Just like my mom did." She moved away and fumbled for her keys in her purse, which seemed even more bottomless with the keys buried in the deep, dark recesses. Abbie didn't want to offend her but also didn't want Joan to get the wrong idea.

A slightly pleasant flutter had started to develop in Abbie's stomach and she felt flushed. *What idea do I want to give her? I'm probably sending some very mixed messages. What the hell am I doing?*

Abbie finally got the car door opened and got in. Joan leaned over and kissed her cheek.

"I had a great day, Abbie." She straightened up and stepped back to let Abbie close the door. Abbie rolled down the window.

"I did too, thanks for everything," Abbie busied herself starting the car and waved absently out the window. She stole a glance over her shoulder as Joan sauntered back to her little red sports car. "See you on Saturday for girl's night out," she called over her shoulder.

Abbie's mind was racing, and so was her heart. What was that all about? Was she still drunk? Should she even be driving? It had been several hours since lunch and Abbie hadn't had anything to drink since. She should be fine to drive. It wouldn't do for a cop's wife to be pulled over for a DUI, especially with Conrad vying for promotion. As she pulled away from the curb, she angled the rearview mirror towards her and half-turned. She couldn't turn far enough to actually see her new tatt and still stay on the road so she gave up. *I'll have a look when I get home.* It was covered with a bandage anyways and Bill had told her to keep it on for a day or two and then put antibiotic ointment on it every night for two weeks.

She turned on the car stereo, leaned her elbow out the window and let the breezes float in around her. She felt her alter ego burst forth as it always did when she was alone in the car with the stereo blasting. She was a diva on stage belting out *Gypsies, Tramps and Thieves* right along with Cher, one of her all-time favorite female vocalists. A smile crept onto her face like a cloud moving away to reveal a brilliant ray of sun. *I'm such a rebel!*

As she pulled in her driveway, reality sunk in and the cloud billowed back. She hoped no one was home. She wasn't ready to tell them yet. She was relieved to see that Conrad's car wasn't there. The kitchen door was unlocked so one of the boys must be home. Abbie pulled her hair over the bandage and hoped it didn't show. She tiptoed up the stairs and headed down the hall to her room.

"Mom, is that you?" Winston popped his head out of his bedroom door.

"Yeah honey, how was your golf game?" She kept walking hoping he would go back to what he was doing but he followed her into her bedroom and sat on the bed."

"Great. How was your day?" He looked at her with his penetrating blue eyes. She knew he wasn't going to bring up the night before. He was just too considerate for that, but she could sense he was concerned. He was her sensitive child for sure.

"I had a nice day. Went to lunch with Joan." Abbie turned so that her right side was away from him.

"I really liked her, she was cool," Winston said. "And hot too."

"So you said and I agree, she *is* cool and fun," Abbie wandered into her bathroom.

"What's that on your neck?" Winston called after her.

"Oh, it's nothing." Abbie tried to think fast. "I got a fly bite and it's gotten infected. Okay, I'm going to take a shower and I'll be done in a bit. Want to order pizza for dinner?"

"Sure thing . . . any requests?"

"No, order whatever you like." The food ploy had worked again. Abbie closed the bathroom door and turned on the shower. She heard Winston leave and close the bedroom door behind him.

CHAPTER 7

The week went by fairly uneventfully and since Conrad had done a double shift early in the week and had been working nights and sleeping during the day he hadn't noticed the new addition of Abbie's body art and she couldn't bring herself to tell him just yet. She kept the bandage on longer than she needed to and then blew dry her hair forward. Fortunately, it was small enough that her hair easily covered it.

It was Friday night and the boys were out, Conrad was working and Abbie had an evening to herself. *Ah bliss!* She quickly threw on a load of laundry that had gone forgotten for a few days. The boys wouldn't have any clean underwear left if she didn't. Then she tossed a bag of popcorn in the microwave, poured herself a glass of wine, popped *Rent* into the DVD player and planned to sing along to every song without being teased.

She climbed into bed well after midnight and was asleep when Conrad got home but she felt him as he climbed in beside her. She snuggled back against him into their favorite spooning position.

Not long after, Abbie awoke to the pin pricks of heat

crawling all over her body like a thousand red ants leaving tiny, scorching footprints behind.

Conrad started like he had been burned. "Jesus, you're burning up!" He held her at arm's length. "Are you okay? It's like a furnace just switched into overdrive."

"I know. Think how it feels from the inside," Abbie replied despondently as she flapped the covers to try to get some respite yet knowing it was going to get worse. "I'm going to get some air." She climbed out of bed and padded in her bare feet to the door.

"Want me to come with you?" Conrad asked, a tinge of concern appearing in his voice.

"No . . . But thanks. I won't be long."

"It was raining when I came in and it's cooled down a lot tonight. Your raincoat's by the back door. You don't want to get a chill."

"Don't worry, I'll be fine." Abbie's voice had an edge of irritation. She couldn't help it but with a herculean effort, softened her tone. "I'll be back in a while."

She tiptoed past the boys' rooms and crept down the stairs and into the kitchen, slipped on her crocs and her raincoat but left it unzipped to let in the cool air. She went off to the left, down the side of the house to the driveway, avoiding looking at the back gate, still not having ventured to the other side of the fence since the frying pan incident.

She walked briskly down the sidewalk to make the best use of the air filtering in and around her body, while the sweat poured down her back, and speckled her upper lip. Rounding the first turn on the crescent where they lived, she glanced back at Bess's house. Her lights were off so hopefully Bess was sleeping. Abbie didn't need the neighborhood gossip talking about her wild walk in the middle of the night. She made a quick turn onto the cul de sac that jutted off to the right and headed for the familiar pathway between two houses that led to the next street. The wind was kicking up so she dug her hands into her pockets. Her hand felt the small cylinder of pepper spray that she had carried while the neighborhood was being terrorized by that awful pit bull. Guess she didn't have to worry about that any more. She felt her stomach do a flip-flop and wondered again if she was going to get into trouble for that.

She heard a rustle in the bush just ahead and stopped dead in her tracks. A man in a trench coat and cap pulled down low over his eyes stepped out. Abbie gripped the pepper spray tighter as he approached. *Oh my God! He's going to flash me! What an asshole!* A wave of anger overtook her as she lunged towards him and sprayed him full in the face. Abbie's foot hit a slippery spot and her tread-less crocs made her slide, continuing her forward momentum. She unavoidably body-slammed him and tackled him to the ground. He screamed. His hands flew to his eyes as she came down on top of him.

Petrified, Abbie pushed herself away as her attacker's arms flapped around his face, his unseeing eyes becoming beat red from the spray. She scrambled to her feet, her anger melting into fear that he would retaliate. She turned and ran as fast as she could to the safety of her own back yard before he could regain his sight.

She slammed the gate closed and sat on her the back stairs until her heart stopped feeling like it was beating out of her chest. She couldn't tell Conrad what had happened. He would go ape-shit and all protective and 'cop-like' on her and run after the guy. Then he would lecture her on how she really shouldn't have gone out on her own; and he should have gone with her; and what was she thinking... She could hear it now and it would be too much for her to deal with on top of it all. She had taken care of it, right? The flasher certainly would not have seen which way she went so couldn't know where she lived. She had already stirred up enough shit for a lifetime so she decided to keep yet another little secret to herself. She figured the flasher had learned his lesson for the day.

She hung her raincoat up and closed and locked the back door behind her then tiptoed up the stairs, skirting the center of the fifth step up that always creaked like the floorboard in the hall, quietly crept into the bedroom and slid in beside Conrad.

"How was your walk," he mumbled, half asleep.

"It was fine," she hoped she didn't sound as breathless as she felt and that her still pounding heart wasn't vibrating the bed. "The rain stopped and the fresh air felt good... and, Conrad?"

"Hmmmm ... "

"Thanks for being so understanding."

She need not have worried. Conrad was quiet and his breathing slowed to a familiar rhythm. He was already asleep. Abbie rolled over and tried to go to sleep, jealous of his ability to fall asleep at the drop of a hat. It was a good thing with his job. He had to get sleep whenever he had some rare downtime. She usually complimented him on it. Tonight, it just irritated her.

CHAPTER 8

Abbie woke up to breakfast-making sounds coming from the kitchen. Conrad had already gotten up and must be putting the coffee on. She yawned and stretched away the stiffness. Then the memory of the night before came flooding back.

She hoped the flasher hadn't reported the incident. If he did, Conrad would surely hear about it as soon as he got to the station since it happened right in his neighborhood. He would easily put two and two together and then the interrogation would start. He wasn't working until later and by that time she would be at Rachel's getting ready for their night out.

Actually, she would head over as soon as she could pack a bag. Joan was spending the whole weekend at Rachel's so she would already be there. Maybe they'd have the Bailey's out. Abbie, pulled on a pair of shorts and a t-shirt, grabbed her new outfit and make-up bag and stuffed them into an overnight bag.

She came out of her bedroom and practically collided into Trevor in the hallway headed to the bathroom.

"Hey Mom, you okay?" Trevor looked down at the overnight bag in her hand. "Where're you going?"

"Oh, just to Rachel's. We're going out tonight so I'm going to stay over with her so we can share a cab. I'll be back tomorrow. Good luck with your exam today. It's the last one so you must be excited," she called over her shoulder as she headed down the stairs.

Conrad and Winston both turned quizzical looks towards her as she came into the kitchen.

"Morning Mom, want some coffee?" Winston held up the coffee pot he had in his hand. He must have just poured himself a cup.

"Hi hon. Did you sleep okay?" Conrad kissed her on the cheek she offered him distractedly. "I must have been dog tired. I barely remember you coming back to bed. How was your walk?"

"My walk? Oh, it was fine. Win, thanks but I'm on my way out so I'll grab one on the way." Abbie tugged at her hair to make sure her new tattoo was covered. She had finally taken the bandage off realizing it looked even more conspicuous. Her hair covered it just fine as long as it was pulled forward. She didn't need the lecture just yet.

"On the way? Where are you going?" Conrad stood between Abbie and the door so she had little choice but to stop and have the conversation.

"To Rachel's. Remember I told you that we were doing a girl's night tonight and I was going to stay over with her? You're working tonight anyways so you said you didn't mind."

"Oh right. Why so early?"

"Um . . . you know us girls. Any opportunity to have a gab session." She skirted around him, grabbed a buttered bagel that he had left on the counter, took a bite and said a muffled, "Later guys," with a wave over her shoulder.

Abbie practically ran to her car and started it before she

even had the door closed. She plugged in her hands-free while backing out of the driveway and punched Rachel's number on speed-dial. She jammed it into first gear and squealed the tires.

"Abbie, it that you?" Rachel answered the phone. "What was that noise?"

Abbie giggled, surprised at how unpredictable her emotions were. One minute she was full of anxiety the next she was laughing. "I just peeled out of the driveway, laid rubber, as the boys would say... I'm on my way."

You're coming now? Jeez, aren't you the eager beaver?"

"Uh, hmmm . . . sorry, is that okay?"

"Of course it is. Joan's just getting a shower and I've made a fresh pot of coffee. Get your butt over here sista!"

"I may need a nap this afternoon before we go out but I'm on my way! I'll have to borrow some make-up too. I was in such a hurry to get out of the house and I think I grabbed the wrong cosmetic bag."

"Not to worry. I'm sure I'll have anything you need. You did remember your new outfit though, right?"

"Of course! It's been sitting on my dresser all week but I'm sure it'll probably need to be ironed. I've been looking forward to this since last Saturday."

"Me too, see you shortly."

"Already halfway there! And Rachel? I've got another doozy of a story."

JOAN AND RACHEL SAT, mouths agape, as Abbie recounted her flasher in the bushes story.

"Holy shit! You really showed him, didn't you? You go girl!" Joan high-fived her.

Rachel took Abbie's hands in hers and gave them a

squeeze. "Well, the most important thing is you're okay. But why didn't you tell Conrad and report it to the police?"

"I don't know. You know how Conrad is. He'd be all 'take control' and 'no one hurts my woman' and I just didn't want to deal with it. He already thinks I'm going crazy."

" I guess so . . . your karma is a little out of whack these days, isn't it?" Rachel said trying to lighten the mood.

"Isn't that the truth? You're so lucky your symptoms are so much milder."

"I've been taking Black Cohosh. I read somewhere it helps. I'm not sure if it does or not but I'm definitely not flashing as bad as you are and I'm not really that irritable. Maybe you should give it a try. I know you don't like taking pills, but it's a natural herb.

"Maybe . . . we'll see."

"Okay, so what about this guy? You really should have reported it Abbie."

"I know, I know. Anyways, I'm sure the guy just took off so it would have been too late by the time the police arrived and I would have wasted their time."

"But still. What if this guy hurt someone?"

"Hmmm . . . I didn't think about that. But, you know, I didn't get a good look at him so couldn't give a positive ID anyway. It was raining and I was having one of my moments and he came out of nowhere. I just sprayed and ran."

"Well, it's over now and you're okay and it's just us girls all weekend!" Joan piped in. "What say we get those face masks on and do our nails so they'll have plenty of time to dry. I can't wait to see you in that great outfit we got you last weekend." Joan winked at Abbie.

"Oh come on! You're going to make me blush."

"I hope so. You're gorgeous when you turn pink . . . even when it's a hot flash."

"Come on Joan. Stop flirting," Rachel laughed. "Abbie's

straight as a pin. There will be no converting my friend. We'll find someone else for you tonight."

"I can't convert anyone who doesn't want to be, honey," Joan smiled conspiratorially at Abbie and gave her a pinch as she walked by.

Abbie squealed and swatted Joan's hand. "Sorry, you're barking up the wrong tree," she smiled. "Now, behave yourself!" Abbie was enjoying the flirtation even though she knew it wouldn't go anywhere.

"Well, I managed to talk you into getting a tattoo, didn't I?"

"Holy Shit! You did what?" Rachel scanned Abbie's body. "Where is it? Does Conrad know? Oh my God, what did he say?"

Abbie laughed and pulled her hair up so Rachel could see. "I haven't told him yet. What do you think?"

"It's actually quite nice. When did you do it and how did Joan talk you into it?" Rachel scowled at Joan. "You're going to get me in trouble with Conrad!"

"Oh come on! That was the whole point. Abbie and I had lunch this week and we talked about letting go and living a little," Joan explained. "I asked her when the last time was that she did anything without checking in with her husband first and she couldn't remember." Joan crossed her arms looking satisfied. "Now she has."

"Just remember, she's still married and we're not... there's a reason for that," Rachel shook her head. "Abbie and Conrad are happily married . . . and, don't you forget it!"

"Okay, truce! Rach, let's just get these facials going," Joan winked at Abbie. "I don't care what anyone says. I think it's a great tattoo."

"You're incorrigible. But I do think it's pretty cool too," Rachel pulled Abbie closer to have a better look.

"I love it," Abbie agreed and tilted her head to accommodate Rachel's up close and personal examination. "I just hope Conrad doesn't get mad."

"So, where's the face mask stuff? I'll start getting it ready," Joan picked up the empty coffee mugs. "We should probably do it in the kitchen."

"Good idea. It's in my bathroom under the sink."

Abbie, Rachel and Joan spent the rest of the afternoon in contented girly bliss. They primped and sang along to the dulcet tones of Sarah McLachlan and Melissa Etheridge with a little Shania Twain thrown in to set the party mood; and after a long, leisurely nap in Rachel's sun room, stretched like a cat with the afternoon sunbeams pouring in on her, Abbie was more than ready to party.

CHAPTER 9

Abbie and Rachel had no idea where Joan was taking them but she was adamant that she take the lead. Even after she gave the taxi driver the name, Abbie still didn't have a clue.

"It's been so long since I've been to a dance bar I'm not sure I remember how to act," said Abbie uncertainly, shifting on the seat and trying to stretch her skirt further down towards her knees. She didn't remember it being so short when she bought it. If there was anything remotely resembling a hem she would have considered letting it down.

"Stop fidgeting! You look incredible." Joan playfully slapped Abbie's hand away from her skirt and clinked her plastic cup against the one she held tightly in her hand. "Don't worry, you'll love it!" Joan had insisted they take some 'roadies' and had made a pitcher of cosmopolitans just before they walked out the door. A little pre-lubrication to kick start the party, she said.

"I'm so psyched I can't stand it," Rachel slung her arm over Joan's neck. "Take good care of us now. We're a little out of practice."

Abbie rested her head on the back of the seat and closed her eyes. She would have to slow down a bit on the drinking or she might not make it to the first stop. Joan launched into a diatribe of advice.

"Now, the first place we'll hit is more like a lounge. The dance bars don't get going until much later. I know the bartender and she makes a mean kamikaze."

"I don't even know what that is but it sounds dangerous," Rachel took another swig of her cosmo.

Abbie opened her eyes and stole a glance at the tattoo on the back of Joan's neck. She had only just noticed it when they were getting ready earlier. She wondered why Joan hadn't 'unveiled' it when she talked Abbie into getting hers. Abbie thought the angel wings on Joan's ankle was the only tattoo she had. Joan was now shifted a bit sideways facing slightly towards Rachel so Abbie was able to study it without being obvious. It was the first time she had seen it in full as Joan usually wore her hair down. Tonight it was in a flattering upsweep fastened with a multicolored, randomly geometric, tortoise shell clip.

Even as a fairly new tattoo fan, Abbie could appreciate that this one was a beautiful piece of art. It was a depiction of an angel, with wispy wings and soft edges in hues of blues and pinks with her eyes raised to the sky (or towards the top of Joan's head). As Abbie studied the intricacies of the tattoo she realized that the sweet, ethereal angel had two sharp horns poking out of her curly golden hair and on closer inspection, she was gripping a squirming serpent in her right hand, from which long, red nails sprung.

Abbie gasped. Rachel and Joan had been in a boisterous conversation, planning the evening's escapades and stopped and looked at her.

"What's wrong Abs?" Rachel asked.

"Uh, nothing... just sneezed." She figured Joan probably

had a dark side but she really didn't want to know about it so she tore her eyes away from the disturbing image and downed her cosmo. She tried to stroke down the hairs that were standing on end on the back of her neck and ignored the unreasonable feeling of doom that enveloped her. *It's just hormones.*

"Here we are . . . stop number one!" Joan paid the taxi driver and they all spilled out and headed into *Rick's Place*. It was loosely based on the bar that Humphrey Bogart owned in the movie, *Casablanca*. It was one of Abbie's all-time favorite movies so she forced herself to relax, soaking in the mellow atmosphere.

"What a great spot," Abbie took in the elegant tables set with ivory lace tablecloths and single rose bud vases. The tables sat on tiered platforms and all faced a stage with rich, red bunting and curtains with gold tassels. A piano player just off to the side was playing a little Billy Joel, a more modern day Sam who was the entertainer at Rick's nightclub in the movie. She resisted walking over and telling him to 'play it again'. Joan led them straight to the bar.

"Hey Jami! How's business? I've brought you some new victims... I mean customers." Joan laughed and leaned across the bar and gave Jami a peck on the cheek. "These are my best girls, Rachel and Abbie and we'll have a round of your famous Kamikazes."

"Nice to meet you ladies. Three of my best Ks comin' right up!"

"What's in it?" Rachel pulled her stool closer to the bar and peered over the edge to see what Jami was gathering together for her creations.

"It's usually Cointreau, vodka, lime juice and lime but Jami adds something a little special but she won't tell me what it is." Joan stood with her hands on her hips.

"You can stand there glaring at me all you want. I'm still not telling." She turned her back to block the girls' view.

Abbie looked longingly at the long, silky blond hair that spilled down below Jami's waist. Every time Abbie had tried to grow her hair past her shoulders she just got terrible split ends and had to trim it up and start all over again. She was so glad she'd had her roots done last week when they all went to the salon. Salt 'n pepper sprouting out and topping off her 'summer wheat' colored hair wouldn't be very attractive. She was feeling very self-conscious around all this beauty. Jami was wearing a hot little long-sleeved number, feigning modesty until you saw that the entire back was cut out and it ended in the micro-ist of miniskirts Abbie had ever seen. The outfit was completed with tall, black, shiny platform boots.

"So, it looks like there's going to be a show," Abbie popped a few bar snacks into her mouth. They hadn't eaten much before they left Rachel's, as they were too excited. She knew she'd have to get something into her stomach or she'd be in trouble.

"Only the best damn drag show in town," Jami said proudly over her shoulder.

Abbie almost choked on her peanut. "Drag show?" So much for the 'mellow' atmosphere.

"Oh my God Joan. Nothing like jolting us out of our mundane, mommy caravanning to school, making dinner, laundry-doing, comfort zones," Rachel said. "I guess I should have expected something kooky knowing you."

"Ladies . . . tequila shots, on the house!" Jami plunked down three shot glasses, a plate of lemons and a shaker of salt and proceeded to line up their volatile Kamikaze cocktails in behind like soldiers... armed and dangerous.

"Good lord, if I drink those you'll have to have to carry me out of here!" Abbie shook her head about to decline.

"Oh, come on. Live a little! Tonight's our night and the word no is not in our vocabulary," Joan slid the shot glasses over.

Abbie sighed and reached for one of the glasses. "I'm sure I'm going to regret this but what the hell... you only live once, right?" She licked the skin between the knuckles of her index finger and thumb sprinkled on a dusting of salt.

Rachel grinned. "I think this is what we were doing when we first met at college a hundred years ago."

"I believe so . . . guess I never forgot how to do one of these. Bottoms up!"

"You ladies might want to grab a table so you'll have a better view before all the good seats are gone. The place is starting to fill up." Jami reached for Joan's hand. "And, I hope to see you when I get off later."

"Well, after the show we're headed to *The Orchard* to do some dancing so try to catch up with us there." Ignoring Jami's hand, Joan grabbed her drink and motioned for Rachel and Abbie to follow. She led them to the last table that was empty in the front row, smack dab in the middle. *We'll certainly have a great view, up close and 3D.*

"I'm going to powder my nose. You guys stay here and hold the table and I'll be right back."

"Are you having fun yet?" Rachel leaned over closer to Abbie so she could hear her. The music had been cranked up, a little Bette Midler to get everyone in the right mood.

"More fun than I've had in a long time and I haven't had a hot flash for hours. Or, maybe I've got a perma flush from the alcohol."

"Whatever works!" They clinked glasses and Joan re-joined them just as the house lights were dimming. Abbie thought her eyes were looking a little glassy and wondered exactly what type of 'powdering' Joan was doing to her nose. She found herself wondering what it might feel like to get high. Being married to a cop, there were no drugs in her life but she couldn't help being curious.

"Ladies and gentlemen, butches and queens, Rick's Place proudly presents, for your listening and viewing pleasure, 'Divas on Parade'.

Out strutted Bette Midler, Liza Minelli, Barbra Streisand, Dion, Donna Summer, Cher, and Madonna all singing a choral version of Helen Reddy's "I am Woman, Hear me Roar".

Abbie leaned towards Joan, put her hand on her knee and cupped her hands around her ear and whispered loudly, "It's hard to believe they're men. They're so beautiful. And, realistic. Especially Cher."

"I know. That's my friend Simon. He'll most likely join us later. He loves to dance." Joan put her hand over Abbie's and squeezed. Abbie was feeling no pain and as Joan started caressing her hand under the table, she didn't pull hers away. She liked how it felt. If Rachel noticed she didn't let on. She was too busy singing along with Barbra's "New York State of Mind".

The whole crowd sang along as the Divas sang every popular show tune and a pop disco-diva mash-up that would have put TV's Glee to shame. Abbie lost count of the costume changes but, scanning the room every so often, realized that the show off-stage was just as entertaining as the one on-stage. At one point Abbie puzzled over two familiar faces she saw in the crowd. *I can't believe I would know anyone here.* Then, the realization dawned on her and she caressed the memorial to her mother that snuggled on her neck, just below her hairline, in back of her ear. It was Bill and Mike from the tattoo parlor, in all their leather-clad glory, standing arm and arm and belting it out right along with the rest of the crowd. They spied Abbie at the same time and both waved to her. Abbie waved back enthusiastically, swaying her hips in time with the music. She let out a gasp and a then a giggle as Bill did a pirouette and she saw two white orbs peeking out through the cutouts on the back of his leather chaps.

"Hey girls, look! There are the guys from the tattoo shop," Abbie yelled in her friends' direction. "I can't believe the outfits."

Joan laughed and waved over to them.

For the finale, Simon/Cher reached down to Joan and pulled her up on the stage and motioned for Abbie and Rachel to join them in the kick line. They linked arms in a long can-can line, doing the high kick while they all belted out, "It's up to you - New – York - Neewww York!" When the music ended the applause was deafening. Abbie, Joan and Rachel all took a deep bow alongside the Divas.

Their adrenalin was well and truly pumping and they were ready to keep on dancing. Holding hands, the three gals ran out to the sidewalk in front of *Rick's* and flagged down a taxi.

"*The Orchard*, please!" Joan gasped, trying to catch her breath as they all tumbled into the back seat giggling.

"That was so much fun," Abbie and Rachel squealed in unison. "I've never seen a drag queen so close up before," Abbie added. "Actually, I've only ever seen one on TV. You know the movie with Robin Williams?"

"Yeah, 'The Bird Cage'. Great movie. Well, Simon will probably come dancing in drag so you'll be able to get an even better look," Joan laughed.

"What about Jami?" Rachel winked at Joan and nudged her shoulder.

"Oh, we're just friends. I think she'd like something more but I'm just not in that mind-set. I'm not even divorced yet and I'm still trying to get comfortable in the new skin."

"She's friends, we're friends, we're all friends together," Abbie warbled in a childlike singsong, nursery rhyme.

"Wow... are you drrrunk," Rachel slurred.

"Yeah, and you're sober as a judge," Joan teased.

The taxi pulled up to *The Orchard* and Abbie looked in dismay at the hordes waiting to get in. "Holy shit... look at the line-up."

"Don't worry, I know the bouncer. He'll have us on 'the list'."

"My turn to pay then," Abbie fumbled and yanked on the zipper of her little disco bag. She hadn't used it in so long she'd forgotten that it was broken.

"Don't worry, I got it," Joan waved her hand. "Let's go!"

True to her word, the burly bouncer unclasped the red rope hung between two metal stanchions and lifted it as he saw Joan approaching arm in arm with Rachel and Abbie.

"I have two friends with me tonight. Is that okay Brian?"

"For you, absolutely sugar. You guys have a good time."

Abbie couldn't help thinking that if Joan was such a regular at these places it had to be a lot longer than she was admitting to that she'd been doing the party scene. She seemed pretty comfortable in her skin (and looked pretty good in it too). Abbie felt a flush, not sure if it was the alcohol or a hot flash. She tried to ignore that fact that it could actually be that warm fuzzy feeling that comes over you when you have a physical attraction to someone. She didn't care.

"Come on you guys, let's dance!"

They headed straight for the football field-sized dance floor. It was a throwback from the disco era with a dozen or more disco balls glittering from the ceiling, and square, multi-colored floor lights flashing under their feet. The only difference was the throbbing house music that had become popular in the dance bars. It wasn't Abbie's favorite style of music but she found herself moving to the tribal rhythm and closed her eyes, feeling the vibrations coming up through her feet and settling in her belly. She couldn't remember the last time she let go like this. It was liberating. Tonight, she was just Abbie, the party girl.

Rachel tapped her on the shoulder and yelled into her ear, "I'm going to get a drink of water and sit down for a minute. You want one?"

Abbie shook her head. Why ruin the buzz? Rachel shrugged and went off in the direction of the bar. It was hard to miss. There was only one and it made a swooping arc around the entire dance floor in a huge horseshoe shape. If you were standing at one end of the bar, you could look directly across the dance floor at the other end. The whole bottom floor was dance floor and bar. All the seating was in an upstairs balcony that overlooked the sweaty, writhing throngs getting closer and closer together as more hot bodies pushed themselves into the crowd.

Abbie turned towards Joan and continued to let the music waft around her. She felt like a slow motion mermaid just letting the ebb and flow of the current move her, periodically punctuated by a crashing wave.

Joan grabbed Abbie's hand and led her off the dance floor. Abbie had hit a plateau and was cruising along in a very happy place. She followed Joan into the bathroom and Joan checked under the stalls for feet. She pushed one of the doors open and motioned for Abbie to come in with her. More curious than concerned, Abbie joined her turning sideways so they could both fit. Joan reached into her purse and pulled out a vial with little pink pills, shook one out and held it out to Abbie.

"What is it?" Abbie took it from her and turned it over in her hand and saw a little smiley face stamped on one side.

"It's Ecstasy. Go ahead. It'll keep you going. Otherwise, you'll crash too early."

Abbie shrugged. Just one wouldn't hurt. She popped it in her mouth as Joan did the same then they walked hand in hand out of the bathroom and back out to the dance floor where they saw Rachel and Simon boogieing away. Simon was in his glory, wearing a pink crop top, a tight gold lamé mini skirt with white go-go boots, and swishing a long white feather boa around in the air. He was gorgeous. He wasn't the only man in drag in the place. The Ecstasy was either giving her hallucinations or she was seeing the dancers with more clarity now. The drug seemed to have taken the edge off the alcohol haze. She noticed a few very tall, leggy girls, with adam's apples jutting from their throats and a couple others with a hint of the 5 o'clock shadow. What a place!

Abbie could see that Rachel was scanning the crowd for them.

"There you are! I thought I'd lost you for a minute," she shouted over the music. "Are you ready to go soon?"

"God no, not yet! We just got here." Abbie twirled around and grabbed Rachel around the waist and spun her around. "I feel fantastic!"

Rachel gave in. "Okay, just a little while longer then."

The DJ had shifted to 70s disco music and the dance floor was a sea of jiving and hustling fanatics and Abbie thought it was probably just like Studio 54 was back in the day. Her kids would be mortified if they could see her. So would Conrad. Abbie's smile got wider as she reminded herself that tonight she was Abbie, the party girl. Not someone's mother. And, not someone's wife. She was allowed just one night, wasn't she? She let herself get totally lost in a wild medley of *Disco Inferno, Stayin' Alive* and Maroon 5's *Moves like Jagger* (a little modern day music to balance the mix).

She didn't want the night to end so when Rachel came to her a few songs later and wanted to call it a night, Abbie still wasn't ready.

"You go ahead. I'll stay with Joan and Simon and get a cab to your place later."

"Are you sure? I'll stay if you want me to." Rachel yawned.

"Don't be silly. I'll be fine!"

"O.K. The key's in the usual place. First one up makes the coffee." Rachel kissed Abbie, Joan and Simon European style on both cheeks, turned and tossed a wave over her shoulder. Abbie turned her attention back to her fellow party 'girls'. She caught Joan eyeing her up and down and danced even more seductively. What harm could it do?

CHAPTER 10

A bbie woke in a fog. She had been having erotic dreams again but they had gotten a lot more intense this time. She heard water running nearby and opened her eyes. This wasn't Rachel's spare bedroom. She rubbed her eyes and propped herself on an elbow. Where was she? Her heart started pounding as shards of memories of the night before jabbed into the dark corners of her muddled brain. She felt nauseous.

She was in a motel room. Oh God! What had she done? She looked at her watch. It was still early. She could sneak out and be back at Rachel's and no one would know the difference. Except... whoever was in the bathroom. She blinked through the haze and fumbled on the nightstand for her glasses. She tried desperately to put the pieces together. Last thing she remembered was dancing with Joan and Simon and then leaving with Joan. Oh crap. It hadn't been a dream . . . or, had it?

Swinging her legs onto the floor she reached down for her dress that was crumpled up next to the bed. She quietly slid her dress over her head, picked up her shoes and grabbed her purse that was on the chair by the door. She carefully turned the knob, opened the door and quietly tiptoed out into the breezeway and scurried to the other side of the parking lot before putting on her shoes at the roadside. God her feet hurt. Each step was a painful reminder of her wild night. It was such a blur. So many gaps. Did she and Joan . . . ? She bent over and vomited.

"Oh God, oh God, oh God," Abbie kept saying over and over again and the tears started rolling down her face and she felt the pin pricks of heat starting in the marrow of her bone. Her face broke out in a sweat and rivulets streamed down her back and under her arms. *I've got to think. I couldn't have slept with her. How do two women even do that? I love my husband. It was a one-time thing.* How was she going to explain this to Conrad? She had to get away and think.

She walked aimlessly for several blocks muttering to herself like a homeless schizophrenic who had forgotten her meds. A four-way traffic signal, blinking red in syncopation, seeped through the dull haze of her brain as she slowed to a stop at the corner. She absent-mindedly looked in all directions, as habit would dictate, not really registering much, and paused to wipe her tears and running nose. There was no traffic for miles. As she completed her scan, her gaze fell on a Greyhound bus station. She should just get on a bus and head out of town. Get far enough away so she could think clearly. She wouldn't have to go for long. Just a day or two. Where should she go? She felt an invisible push towards the entrance. Abbie did a diagonal jaywalk across the street. She yanked open the door, walked in and stared up at the departure board behind the ticket counter.

"Where would you like to go today?"

"Uh, I'm not sure." Abbie's eyes scanned the list of cities to see what was leaving soon and saw the answer to her prayers.

"When's the next bus to Portsmouth?" She managed to choke back the tears and ask the clerk. She had spent many happy summers with her family in Portsmouth and new it like the back of her hand. Those carefree summer days seemed a long way off at this very moment. But, she knew her way around the area and it was somewhere she would feel safe. She could go for a few days and sort out her scattered thoughts.

"Leaves in about half an hour. You okay?"

"Yes, I'm fine. How much for a one-way?"

"That's fifty-seven dollars."

Abbie reached for the disco bag hanging from her shoulder, forced the zipper open and pulled out the cash she had. Joan had paid for pretty much everything the night before so she still had money. She counted out the money and the agent slid the ticket over.

"You can wait in the departure lounge over that way," the clerk pointed across the lobby. "It's around the corner to the right and there are vending machines with soda, coffee and hot chocolate."

I probably look like I need a coffee, thought Abbie.

Much to Abbie's relief, the departure lounge was practically empty. As she dug for some change for a cup of coffee, Abbie watched a young mom deftly change her baby's diaper on one of the long, hard benches. It's amazing what you can manage when you have to. On the other side was a young couple stretched on the floor with their heads resting on over-stuffed backpacks. They were sound asleep. She found a quiet, out of the way corner to wait, her back to the entrance so no one could see her face. She blew on her coffee and took a tentative sip. She hoped she could keep it down.

It would be a few hours before anyone missed her. When Rachel woke up and saw Abbie wasn't there she would probably assume Abbie was with Joan and wouldn't check up until later, knowing how late a night it had been and not wanting to wake them up. Conrad had worked the night shift and would be sleeping. He and the boys thought she had stayed at Rachel's anyways so wouldn't be expecting her until later in the afternoon.

Once they realized she was missing, it wouldn't take Conrad long to figure it out. He was a good cop. In the meantime, she could work out what she would say when she saw him and hope like hell he'd forgive her. She hadn't been herself lately. He knew that. But, just how far his patience would go, she didn't know.

"All passengers for Portsmouth, New Hampshire, please board the bus at position number 3. The bus for Portsmouth will depart in 15 minutes."

Abbie was the first on board and picked a seat at the very back corner so no one would bother her, and hopefully not even notice her. She knew that was hoping for a miracle. Her hair was a tangled mess. A brush wouldn't fit into her party purse so she hadn't brought one. She was sure there were probably mascara smudges under her eyes and she had a run in her stocking. Slouching further down into her seat, Abbie tried to make herself as inconspicuous as possible, hoping she'd be able to sleep the two-hour ride away. Exhaustion seeped into every muscle in her body.

The bus started up and shuddered into reverse. As it backed out of the terminal, Abbie looked out the window as a quiet sob escaped from her lips. She closed her eyes and leaned her head back on the seat. *How the hell am I going to explain this to Conrad?*

She fell into a fitful sleep. Visions of Conrad finding her with Joan filtered in and out of her dreams like serpents winding through a game of snakes and ladders. Visions of Joan beckoning her down a garden path that seemed to be ending at a fiery gate, with people reaching out from the other side, some whose faces were twisted in agony, yet others in some sort of rapturous trance.

She woke up just as the bus was pulling into the station at Portsmouth. She felt even worse. Her head was pounding and her mouth felt like it was filled with dirty socks covered in tiny spikes.

She limped out of the bus station, her feet throbbing in her high heels. She had to find something comfortable to wear. She planned to hike to the old hunting cabin about an hour out of town. It was months before anyone would be using it so she could hole up there and think for a couple of days.

She stood on the sidewalk and looked up and down the street while passersby gave her a wide berth and tried not to stare, confirming her assumption that she must look a mess. *I probably also look like a hooker in this get-up.* It was a small and very conservative town. She knew she stuck out like a sore thumb. She hoped no one would recognize her. It wasn't likely since it had been years since she'd been there and even then the locals and cottagers didn't really socialize.

She looked at the sky in the distance and saw dark clouds forming and could smell the telltale scent of rain in the air and thought she'd better pick up the pace.

Finally, she spied what she was looking for... an Old Navy just a half a block down. She still had almost a hundred bucks. She should be able to get a pair of comfy shoes, a t-shirt and shorts if she stuck to the bargain tables. She lucked out and 20 minutes later she was kitted out and on her way with her party dress and stilettos in her shopping bag. The sales were so great she was even able to stop by the mini-mart and stock up on a few essentials. A cool breeze stroked her face as she stepped out of the store like a reassuring hand. The temperature was hovering in the low 70s so it would be a nice walk through town and hike into the woods.

Abbie wasn't on any timeframe so she took her time. Even

if it rained, it would be refreshing and would keep the crowds away. It had been a while so she didn't know how popular the trail was and hoped her memory would serve her well enough to lead her to the right path. The cut through in the woods could possibly have grown over by now. Then an unsettling thought occurred to her. *What if the cabin wasn't there?* She tossed her shoulders back, determined . . . and decided that it had to be there . . . so she would just push on.

She tried to meditate as she walked. Tried to clear her cloudy mind, inhaling and exhaling deeply through her nose, calming the anxiety that had hatched a hoard of butterflies in her stomach. She concentrated on the wind in the trees... watching as each leaf did its own dance. That was always her favorite thing to do as a child. Watch the nuances of nature with her mother who had been an artist and a single mom during a time that it wasn't so common. She had taught Abbie to look for the story behind every movement in nature. Abbie saw the wind like a complex dance choreography with the currents and gusts lifting each individual leaf in time to the hypnotic rhythm of the crickets. The leaves committing to each gust, trusting it like a ballerina giving in to the strength and skills of her partner. Losing herself in the moment.

Abbie tried to lose herself in the moment. There had to be an upside to this. She hadn't been herself lately. This was a brief dalliance. Totally out of character for her. She would never do it again. She loved Conrad and the boys with all her heart. She'd never see Joan again. She would make a promise to him and hopefully he'd forgive her. She hoped he would forgive her for disappearing too. She just couldn't face anyone yet. She hoped the boys were okay. She hoped they weren't too worried. They probably hadn't even noticed. They were rarely around lately anyway and when they were, they were usually shut up in their rooms, studying, texting or chatting with friends on Facebook or doing whatever teenage boys do. She would call them tomorrow.

Finally, she saw the brown sign with the little hiking man figure on it coming up ahead. According to the sign, she had one mile to go. She picked up the pace and soon saw an arrow pointing into the parking lot at the trailhead. She turned in. There was only parking for about 10 cars but there were none around. Abbie hoped that it meant she wouldn't run into anyone. She started up the trail, which was a ten-mile loop. In her recollection, the break in the path would split off to the right in the opposite direction about halfway around the trail. Then there should be a smaller footpath that led to the hunting cabin. For the first time, she noticed signs along the way that warned hikers to stay to the trail during hunting season. Well, the season didn't start for a few months. She wasn't wearing orange but she shouldn't have to worry about a hunter mistaking her for a deer this time of year.

As her mind raced, she kept her eyes peeled for the break in the brush. She had been walking for about 40 minutes and she knew she could do five miles in less than that so it should be coming up soon.

"There it is!" She said to the squirrels and butterflies within earshot. The spot was sort of marked with a rusty metal rod, like you see inside cement pilings in new construction. The rod had a fluorescent plastic strip of material tied to the top. Not a yellow brick road, but still a welcome pathway.

Abbie turned off the hiking path and picked her way through the overgrown footpath. There were patches that were still fairly clear so she was certain she was headed in the right direction. The woods got thicker but the pathway still cut a swath plenty wide enough for her. After another 20 minutes she saw the clearing and the little cabin. She felt like Gretel, but the cabin wasn't made of gingerbread and she sure hoped there wasn't a wicked witch waiting behind the door for her. She hadn't left breadcrumbs behind either but she knew if he put his mind to it, Conrad could find her. She had told him so many stories about her summers here and he was a cop—soon to be detective. She prayed he would still be happy to be married to her.

She walked the short distance across the clearing to the cabin and the dry grass crunched under her feet. She had seen signs forbidding campfires because of the lack of rain so, even if there was wood in the cabin, she wouldn't be able to make a fire. She knew that the sparks coming from the chimney could land on dry brush and start a serious forest fire. She hoped it wouldn't get too cold when it got dark.

She tried the door and, as she suspected, it wasn't locked. It was part of the hunters' code. It was definitely a brotherhood of trust. There was never much left behind in a hunting cabin anyways so theft wasn't really a concern. As long as the windows and doors were closed to ward off any rampaging raccoons or bears, that took care of the main problems. She turned the knob and pushed the door open and stepped into the cabin. It was exactly as she remembered it. Bare, wooden walls, bunk beds off to the left and a cooler box under the one window at the back. She knew it would be empty. The hunter's code also said that you could use the place at your convenience but bring your own grub, carry your garbage out with you and don't leave anything behind that would attract mice, or even bears. There were candles on the ledge along the wall to the right and a little metal, waterproof canister, which, as Abbie guessed correctly, contained some dry matches.

It was getting late but the sun wouldn't set until well after eight o'clock so she had plenty of light left. She unpacked the few groceries she had and put them in the cooler: a few bottles of water, a small jar of peanut butter, crackers, cheese and a box of granola bars. It dawned on her that Conrad would have no choice but to come and get her. She only had a couple of dollars left on her. It had been a half-baked plan but it was the best one she had. She checked her phone and saw that there were a couple of bars so the signal should be fine when the time was right. She then shut it off to preserve the battery. She'd make the call when she was ready to talk.

She stretched out on the lower bunk and slung her arm over her eyes. It was pretty comfortable. Someone had added a six-inch foam mattress to the wooden platform since the last time she was there. Abbie heaved a deep sigh and finally drifted off into a deep, but troubled sleep.

CHAPTER 11

Abbie woke with a start. There were voices shouting and dogs barking somewhere off in the distance. She had no idea how long she'd been sleeping but her arm was numb from laying on it and her back was stiff from being in the same position.

She rubbed her eyes and reached for her glasses. She looked at her watch. It read one o'clock. She set her glasses back down and looked out the window. It was bright out so it couldn't be one o'clock in the morning. It had to be afternoon. Was it possible that she'd slept almost 20 hours? She shook her arm to try to get the blood flowing again and the pins and needles exploded. Her t-shirt was wet so she must have had a few night sweats or hot flashes, rather, if it was the middle of the day.

She swung her legs off the bed and stretched. She definitely heard voices but couldn't tell how close they were. Voices could carry quite a distance if the wind was blowing in the right direction. She could tell that the dogs were getting closer though. Maybe it was a family on the trail with a dog. But, it was definitely more than one. She hoped it wasn't a group coming to use the cabin. She wasn't quite ready to give it up yet.

She grabbed a bottle of water she had left on the floor next to her, cracked it open and downed it in one go. Along with her fuzzy head, she had that horrible cottonmouth as they had called it in her college days. *Serves me right after drinking so much.*

The cabin was so tiny Abbie could almost reach the door while sitting on the bed. She crossed the short distance, floorboards creaking, opened the door a crack and looked out into the woods. Cautiously, she opened it wider and stepped onto the porch.

The voices were definitely coming closer. Should she hide? No, that would be silly. Wait a minute . . . was that Conrad's voice? It couldn't be. Or, could it? How could he have found her so quickly? She felt a prickling of irritation but then a sense of relief washed over her. She shouldn't be left alone with her own crazy, rambling thoughts too long anyways. She might as well face the music. How could prolonging the agony any further really help?

She smiled nervously waiting to greet her visitors, whoever they were. Her smile wavered as about 10 state troopers, one with a German shepherd on a leash, broke through the bramble, with Conrad in the lead.

Wasn't that a bit much? She wasn't a fugitive or anything. What a waste of resources. What pull did Conrad have with police in a totally different state? Unless he thought she was in danger. Abbie's mind was racing as Conrad broke into a run towards her.

"Please, let me handle this, he called over his shoulder to the troopers."

Conrad almost knocked her over as he pulled her into his arms. "Abbie, thank God we found you! Are you okay?"

"Yes, I'm fine . . . and, I'm so sorry to cause such a kafuffle."

"A kafuffle?" Conrad looked at her incredulously.

"Yeah, how did you convince the entire New Hampshire State police force to come looking for me, canines and all? I've only been gone a little over a day. You figured it out much more quickly than I thought you . . . Um, I was going to call you later to let you know I was fine but, here you are. And . . . I've got to tell you something."

"Tell me what? Abbie, there's a warrant out for your arrest!"

One of the troopers started to come towards them with handcuffs at the ready. Conrad held his hand up. "Please... give us just one minute. Please!"

"What? Arrest for what?" Abbie started to panic. There were still so many blanks in her memory of the night out with Joan and Rachel.

"Abbie, you're wanted on suspicion of murder back home," Conrad caught her just as her knees gave out, and eased her onto the step and sat down next to her. "Your friend, Joan, was found dead in a motel bathroom yesterday morning and you were the one who was last seen with her."

"Oh my God!" Abbie leaned over the side of the step and retched. "What happened? Oh God, Joan's dead? How did it happen? I swear I didn't do anything," she sobbed.

Conrad rubbed her back. "I believe you baby but they're going to have to bring you in. Don't say anything until I get you a lawyer. Abs, you're in huge trouble. You've crossed state lines. This is going to get ugly. Promise me you didn't have anything to do with this."

"No . . . I don't know . . . oh my God." Abbie started crying uncontrollably, gasping for breath as her throat constricted, blocking the bile that rose again, burning her esophagus.

The trooper reached down for Abbie's arm and lifted her from the porch. "You have the right to remain silent," was all Abbie heard as she was led away in handcuffs. The rest was a muffled blur of Miranda rights. Being married to a cop, she could have recited them, line by line herself but the whirring in her head muted his voice. Colors swirled around her, greens rolling into blues like a Monet painting. Abbie realized then that she wasn't wearing her glasses. As she desperately tried to gain her footing and keep up with her escort, panic making her heart beat violently against her chest, she called breathlessly to Conrad over her shoulder. "I don't have my glasses! They're in the cabin."

A helicopter appeared over the tree line and landed in a clearing behind the cabin. In two great strides Conrad caught up to them and put his hand on her shoulder. "Abbie, I'll be following right behind and will meet you at the jail. I'll bring your glasses. And, don't say anything to anybody until I get there. Don't worry, we'll figure this out," Conrad tried to reassure her as he walked alongside her, all of them hunched over under the circling blades overhead. He went as far as he could until the trooper put his arm in front of Conrad and then guided Abbie into the chopper. He got in beside her and closed the door.

The chopper lifted off and Abbie could feel her stomach dropping down to her feet and a feeling of dread enveloped her like thick, black molasses running over a stack of pancakes. She watched out the window as Conrad became smaller and smaller and then disappeared from view as the chopper swerved up and over the treetops. The trooper next to her stared straight ahead, his face set in a grim scowl and didn't say a word the whole flight. It was probably just a few minutes but seemed like an eternity.

The events of the past several months, and especially the last few weeks, came flooding back. Wildly unsettling thoughts running through her post-binge night brain; irrational reactions to mundane daily situations; wild dogs; flashers in the bushes; lesbian friends; getting ink injected under her skin; erotic dreams; boys growing up, not needing her anymore; can't cook; can't think, can't sleep; crevices in her body that have never been there before; water works – sweat pouring from all orifices and tears bursting forth, unstoppable, without warning; isolation; running away from problems; drinking herself to oblivion; doing things that she would never do like taking drugs; pushing Conrad away and then pulling him back in; the list was endless and made Abbie dizzy. She thought she was going to be sick to her stomach again but there was nothing left in it to bring up. The dry heaves started. The trooper looked over at her, disgusted, and passed her an airsick bag. Abbie held it over her face and breathed deeply in and out. She had seen that in a movie before and hoped it was true that it would help calm her down. The wind had kicked up and the chopper was bouncing around. Her stomach was still doing flip-flops and she could feel the foamy bile rising in her throat again but she managed to fight it down. Her racing heart slowed down slightly and her dizziness ebbed a bit. How did this happen? Where was the normal, middle of the road, milquetoast Abbie? She missed her and wanted her back. She preferred the boring mother, wife and volunteer to the wild, tattooed, party girl of the past few weeks that she didn't recognize. Although there were some fun moments this was certainly not one of them. And, what had happened to Joan? She couldn't be dead. Oh God, if only she could remember. *Poor Rachel. She must be having a fit!*

The chopper touched down on the roof of the police station and the trooper grabbed her arm and half dragged her out, pushing her head down to avoid the chopper blades. Abbie turned her now tear-streaked face away from the dust and debris being kicked up as the cop led her handcuffed into the building. He parked her unceremoniously on a bench while she was processed and then led her to a small cell. True to his word, Conrad arrived about an hour later and immediately signed in and came to her in the holding cell of the city jail.

"Okay Abbie, what's going on?" He took both her hands through the bars and looked into her eyes, willing the story out of her. "You had me crazy with worry. Rachel called and said you hadn't shown up at her place so she figured you were home. I was still at the station so I called home and the boys said they hadn't seen you," Conrad rubbed the back of his neck. He stared directly into Abbie's eyes and shook his head sadly. "You've been acting so weird lately, I didn't know what to think. Rachel came down and met me at the station. We were about to file a missing person report when the report about your friend came in," Conrad started pacing in the cramped hallway outside the cell. Abbie could tell he was trying not to get angry. She had seen him like this before but it was usually with one of the boys. "Rachel recognized her name so the connection was made pretty quickly. The motel manager saw you leave and saw the direction you had gone and the rest was easy to figure out since the bus station isn't so far away. There weren't many people that went through at that hour of the morning so the cashier was able to identify you and remembered where you were going."

"I'm so sorry I worried you. But, I swear to you, I didn't kill her." Abbie sat down on a cot in the cell, crossed her legs and hugged a grungy, yellow pillow, to her chest. "How did it happen?"

Conrad pulled a chair up to the bars outside the cell and drew a deep breath. "She was electrocuted."

"Ohhhh . . . " Abbie started crying again. Her heart broke for her new friend. She hadn't known Joan for very long but they had grown close in a short time. She might have been a bit wild but Abbie knew she had a good heart. Or, did have. Abbie groaned and her sobs got louder.

"Okay, calm down honey," Conrad ran his fingers through his hair. "I'm so sorry about your friend but this is such a mess. We've got to figure out exactly what happened and how to get you out of this. Just start from the beginning. Rachel's told me everything up until she left but I want you to tell me from your perspective. And don't leave anything out."

Abbie took a deep, shuddering breath. She wasn't entirely sure where to start. "I'll tell you everything I can remember but to be honest, there are a few gaps. We drank an awful lot and..." Abbie paused.

"And? Go on," Conrad encouraged her to remember. Abbie could tell he was trying to be patient and control his temper. He was rubbing his forehead, which was something he always did when he was upset or puzzled.

"And, I think I took some Ecstasy," she looked at him pleadingly, hoping he wouldn't get mad.

"Oh Abbie. You don't do drugs. What in God's name were you thinking? Why in the hell would you do that?"

"I don't know. I was caught up in it all. I had been drinking and it just happened." Abbie reached for the roll of toilet paper that sat beside the metal toilet in the corner, pulled a long strip off and wiped her nose.

Conrad let out a long, deep sigh and his head dropped into his hands. His shoulders slumped.

"When can I go home?" Abbie's voice was barely audible.

"Home? Well, there's an extradition order out for you from the Massachusetts' prosecutor's office. They'll be here tomorrow to pick you up so you'll have to stay here tonight."

A sob caught in Abbie's throat. "Stay here? Tonight? I don't understand. Are you sure?"

"Yes, and then there will be an arraignment when we get back but probably not until the day after tomorrow so you'll have to stay another night in jail in New Bedford. Hopefully the judge will set bail and release you into my custody. Then, you'll be able to come home."

Abbie was still in shock. She had been somewhat prepared to explain her tryst with Joan and ask Conrad's forgiveness. She wasn't 100 percent sure there had even been one but waking up naked was probably a good indication that something had happened. But it was so much more complicated now. She felt like she had fallen in Alice's rabbit hole and was in a surreal otherworld where nothing was making sense. The room started to spin around her.

"I think I'm going to faint," Abbie moved the pillow away from her face. She suddenly noticed that it smelled like a stagnant frog pond. She closed her eyes and took a few deep breaths until the spinning stopped.

"I've contacted Ben Hurst," Conrad brushed his hand over his cropped hair as he started pacing again. He must have just cut it the day before yesterday, Abbie thought. It was freshly done in his usual brush cut that he did himself and said was so easy to take care of. She knew it was also because it saved money. He thought going to a barber was a waste of money when you could get the shears yourself and do it at home. He'd been cutting the boys hair since they were two years old.

"Who's Ben Hurst?" Abbie asked as she smoothed down her t-shirt and plucked at a loose thread on her shorts, hopelessly trying to be calm.

"He's one of the best criminal lawyers in town. He's making a special trip up here this afternoon to meet with you and get a head start. You need to tell him everything."

"Can we afford him?"

"Abbie, they've literally got you with the smoking gun. You're going to need the best. We'll have to dip into the boy's college fund but this is an emergency."

"We can't do that!"

"We have no choice but don't worry about it. We've been saving since they were born so there's enough there. They both have full rides this year so we'll have time to shore it up again. They'll both be working this summer so they'll just have to start saving their money too. It's about time they started. We can't carry them forever."

"Oh Jesus, the boys," Abbie looked around the cell and looked up to heaven, wondering if it could get much worse. "Do they know?"

"I haven't told them about Joan yet but I'm going to tell them tonight," Conrad threw up his hands. "It'll be all over the news soon enough so it's better if it comes from me."

"I guess so... please tell them I love them."

Abbie stood up and started pacing too...as much as the confines of the tiny cell would allow. She started chewing on the sides of her fingers. It was a nervous habit that she'd never been able to break. Her mother's voice echoed in her head... *Honey, stop chewing your fingers.* Abbie took her hand out of her mouth and wiped it on her shorts. *Oh my God... my mom. She must be rolling in her grave.*

"Abbie, why don't you sit down and tell me the rest," Conrad pointed to the cot and tilted his head, encouraging her to relax. "You'll have to have it all sorted out in your head anyways to tell Ben when he gets here."

Abbie haltingly told Conrad everything she could remember, starting with *Rick's Place* and the drag show and then dancing at *The Orchard*. "We were having so much fun and Joan's such a riot. Or, I mean she was." Abbie hesitated as a fresh batch of tears started gathering in her eyes.

"I know this must be hard, but go on," Conrad reached through the bars and took her hands in his. She gripped his hands like a lifeline in the middle of raging rapids that were dragging her down.

"Well, we were dancing . . . me, Joan, Rachel and Simon."

"Who's Simon?"

"He's Joan's gay friend who we met at the drag show."

"Joan's gay friend?" Conrad was shaking his head. "Just what have you gotten yourself into Abs?"

She felt a flush overtake her body and suffuse her face with heat. Suddenly, her plan to fess up didn't seem so easy. As a cop, Conrad had seen it all but he was the most conservative, traditional, strait laced person she knew. His grandparents were British and with only one generation removed from the UK, he carried a lot of the common traits and was still just as proper as they were.

"I haven't gotten myself *into* anything," Abbie started a little defensively. "I've been having a bit of a rough time lately, you know that, and Rachel and I met Joan and she liked to have a bit of fun, that's all," she trailed off, losing a bit of her bravado.

Conrad gave her a look that pierced right through her. "Abbie, you're not telling me everything, are you?"

"Well, Joan's gay too but I told you that after that first day I met her at Rachel's, remember?"

"Yes, I do remember that but what I want to know is how you wound up drugged out in a motel room with a lesbian who turned up dead. That's what I'm trying to get at." Conrad pulled his hands away and resumed his pacing.

Abbie swallowed hard, trying to regain her composure. "I honestly don't know. We had so much to drink the last thing I remember was going into the bathroom at *The Orchard* with Joan and taking a little pink pill with a smiley face on it. The next thing I remember is waking up in the motel room. My clothes were on the floor and Joan was in the bathroom. Or at least I assumed it was her. I left as fast as I could. I didn't know what else to do. I heard water running so she must have still been alive when I left."

Conrad raked his hands through his hair again trying to process what Abbie had just told him. She held her breath and waited for a reaction.

"I need to get some air," he didn't look at her and almost ran to the end of the corridor. "Guard! Can you open the door please?" His back was still turned to her as door opened. "Ben will be here shortly so I'll meet him upstairs and bring him down to you," Conrad called down the corridor just as the door closed behind him.

Abbie leaned back against the cold brick wall of the cell and closed her eyes. The cold seeped through her back as she felt an icy hand of dread take a grip on her heart.

CHAPTER 12

B en Hurst was a tall but stocky, good-looking man in his fifties, with salt and pepper hair and a very officious manner. He marched purposefully into the cell and took Abbie's hand in a firm grip. They were calloused hands, not what you'd expect from a white-collar worker. Obviously he had hobbies that were a little more physically rigorous.

He was alone. "Where's my husband?" Abbie took a tentative look behind Ben and down the empty hallway.

"I told him to go get a bite to eat. I need your undivided attention. It's best if he's not here to distract you. We have a lot to accomplish before the arraignment the day after tomorrow."

He took out a pen and legal pad and pulled the chair up close. "I'm afraid I have some bad news."

"You mean worse that being charged with a murder I didn't commit?" Abbie shot back.

"I'm afraid so. They've added another charge . . . Mark Waller was found dead right around the corner from your place about a week ago and there's a witness who can put you at the scene."

"Wait . . . what? I don't understand. Who says they saw me and where? And who the hell is Mark Waller?"

"You don't know him?"

"No, the name doesn't sound familiar at all," Abbie shook her head slowly, letting this new information sink in. "Who is he?"

"He was Joan's husband."

"Joan's husband? I don't understand."

"The prosecutor is saying you killed him in a jealous rage. That you and Joan were having an affair."

"What? No! That's absolutely not true. I've never even met Joan's husband. I don't think I had ever even heard her say his name."

"But you were having an affair with her?"

"No... I mean not really. Jeez, I don't know. We flirted a little but that was all."

"What about the motel?"

"It was the only time and I don't even know if anything happened. I blacked out. We had been drinking an awful lot."

"Well, they're going to say you had been having an affair and that Joan's husband, who was distraught at their break-up, was following you, wanting to talk and you killed him because you were worried he was going to tell your husband."

"That's absurd," Abbie began then the light dawned. "Oh God, the flasher. I went for a walk and some guy came out of the bushes. I thought he was going to flash me so I pepper sprayed him."

"That's it? You pepper sprayed him? The guy's head was bashed in with a rock. They're going for first degree murder."

"A rock? No, I just pepper sprayed him and ran. That was it. And, I didn't know until just now that he was Joan's husband."

Ben's head was bent over his legal pad busily taking notes.

"You believe me, don't you?"

"Yes, I do but you'll have to give me more to go on. We'll have to convince a jury."

———

THE DAY of the arraignment dawned cold and dreary. Conrad brought Abbie a navy blue pants suit with a pink blouse and blue pumps to wear. He looked like he'd been up all night.

"Conrad, I'm so sorry," was all she could manage before her throat closed. He looked so forlorn. She was so used to him being so tough and in control. Seeing him like this made her stomach lurch and her heart ache for him. She wanted him to be angry. To lash out at her. His reaction was almost too hard to bear.

"Abbie, I just don't understand. Aren't you happy with me? With our life? With the boys?"

"Oh God Conrad! I love you and the boys with all my heart. I don't know what came over me. It'll never happen again, I swear."

"Let's get through this first and then we'll talk some more about it."

"Okay," Abbie tried a weak smile and reached for Conrad's hand.

"I'll have to meet you at the courthouse. They'll be bringing you with a police escort so I'll see you there," he leaned over and brushed her cheek with his lips and was gone.

She couldn't imagine how tough this was on him. She knew that some very close friends of his were working on the case. He had taken a leave but was still informally involved and had told her about all the evidence that had been gathered against her. He assured her it was all circumstantial, but many cases were won solely on circumstantial evidence. The burden of proof was supposedly on the prosecution but Abbie couldn't deny being in both places at the time of Joan and Mark's deaths and knew how suspicious it all looked.

On the way to the courthouse Abbie played the scene from the night Joan's husband had died over and over again in her head. She remembered it clearly. Not like the night Joan died, which was still a blur. She knew she hadn't hit him with a rock. Maybe when he fell he hit his head. It was raining and slippery. Wouldn't that be a plausible explanation? He had come out of nowhere and to Abbie he had looked threatening. Of course, late at night, in the dark and in the rain anyone would look menacing.

She wished she could remember what happened in the motel. There was no way she could have hurt Joan. Conrad had said Joan had been electrocuted? What a horrible way to go. Abbie couldn't remember seeing the interior of the bathroom, let alone any type of electrical appliance but the report said a hairdryer was found in the bathtub with the body. So, it could have been an accident. Or, even suicide. She prayed Ben was as good as they said he was. Conrad had told her he had a stellar track record so she felt she was in good hands.

She walked into the courtroom and immediately saw Conrad and Rachel sitting side by side in the front row. She was relieved to see that Trevor and Winston weren't there. Conrad said they had taken the news quite well but had tons of questions. Most of all, they wanted to know when she would be home. Abbie's heart melted when he told her that. Her boys were her life. And, she knew deep down in her heart, that that was okay. She wanted that life back and couldn't believe she had ever looked longingly at Rachel and Joan's new-found freedom, thinking that it might be better.

As she was escorted to the defendant's table a strong waft of lemon scented disinfectant swirled around her, the previous night's attempt to scrub away the sweat of the criminals who sat there before her. Abbie shuddered at the thought of being lumped into such a category and sat down heavily next to Ben. She turned around and Rachel leaned over the railing that separated them to hug her tightly.

"It's going to be okay," Rachel sniffed and gave Abbie a squeeze. "I know you couldn't have done this."

"Thanks for being here Rach," Abbie cast a look at Conrad but he was staring straight ahead, watching as the judge came into the courtroom. She knew he would be struggling with his own demons right now and she hoped he (and ultimately she) would win the battle. The stark florescent lighting of the courtroom emphasized the dark shadows under his eyes. Her breath caught in her throat as she felt the deep dismay of what she was putting him through grinding away in her gut.

"All rise. The Honorable Courtney Rayburn, presiding."

"You may be seated," the judge invited.

"We lucked into a female judge," Ben leaned over and whispered in Abbie's ear. "That's at least one thing on our side. She's likely to be more sympathetic."

Courtney Rayburn didn't look like the sympathetic type to Abbie. Of course, it was hard not to look harsh in a black robe. Her long dark hair pulled back and rolled into a knot at the nape of her neck didn't soften her look, which was accented further by thick, black-rimmed glasses, which only added to the severity.

It could have been Judge Rayburn's twin sitting at the table next to them. The county prosecutor, Kate Masters, was just as stern looking and had more files and notepads stacked in front of her than Ben did. Abbie felt a trickle of sweat run down the length of her back, wondering what could possibly be in all those files.

"Will the defendant please stand," Judge Rayburn interrupted Abbie's thoughts. "How do you plead?"

"Not guilty, Your Honor," Abbie managed to get out, her

right hand gripping the edge of the table. Her knees were shaking so bad she thought she would crumble onto the floor any minute. Ben stood next to her with his hand on her back to steady her.

"Defense requests bail of $50,000 and that she be released into the custody of her husband who is a well-respected, decorated law enforcement officer," Ben added.

"Prosecution?"

"Your Honor, this defendant has been charged with two counts of murder. We believe she is a flight risk as she already fled the state immediately after the second murder. We request that no bail be set and that she is remanded into custody."

Abbie's heart fell into her stomach.

"Fair enough. There will be no bail and the defendant is remanded into custody. Hearing date set for two weeks from today. Next case," Judge Rayburn banged her gavel.

Ben was putting his notes into his briefcase. "Well, that's it then."

"What do you mean, 'that's it'?" Abbie felt the panic rising. She reached behind her back, searching for Conrad's hand.

"It's time to get down to work is what I mean," Ben answered, snapping his briefcase shut. "The prosecution has skipped the Grand Jury so they obviously feel very confident in their case. I'll see you tomorrow and we'll start building yours." He gave her shoulder a reassuring squeeze. "Try to get some sleep, okay?"

Yeah right. Sleep. In a two-by-four cell with a paper-thin pillow and a scratchy wool blanket that smells like wet dog.

"It's going to be okay hon," Conrad said, not very convincingly as Abbie was led away in cuffs.

THAT NIGHT CONRAD dropped by briefly to bring her some fresh underwear and a new toothbrush. He didn't stay long and mumbled something about her needing a good night sleep. Abbie could tell he was still grappling with the whole situation. She knew that being embroiled in a murder case like this wasn't going to help his chances of a promotion. She would just have to let him work through it and pray that she would be found innocent and that her family wouldn't wind up getting hurt in any way. She desperately wanted to get back to normal.

She hadn't prayed in a long time but it was probably a good time to start again. She turned her eyes up towards heaven and prayed like she'd never prayed before and hadn't done much of over the past several years. Abbie had basically turned her back on organized religion a long time ago but believed in her heart that God didn't need you to sit in a hard pew, listening to someone else preaching the 'Word of the Lord' for an hour every week in order to be a good person. She did believe that there was a greater being and He or She was called so many different things the world over, but ultimately, that everyone prayed to the same benevolent God. She believed that you could pray from wherever you were and she hoped that God felt the same way and could hear her praying from a little 10 by 10 jail cell in New Bedford, Massachusetts.

Ben had asked her to come up with a list of character witnesses. She didn't want to drag anyone else into this mess who didn't need to be but Ben insisted it was going to be the cornerstone of the case. All through a very sleepless night, Abbie worked on a mental list of people to suggest, crossed them off, added them again and slotted them in columns in the gray matter corners of her brain . . . for sures, maybes, and no friggin' ways.

CHAPTER 13

"You look like death warmed over," Ben commented through the bars as the guard unlocked Abbie's cell.

"Thanks. That's just what I needed," Abbie glared. "I couldn't sleep. I can't stay here another night... isn't there anything you can do? I'm going to go crazy in here! I didn't do anything . . . please!" Abbie's voice rose, tinged with a hint of hysteria.

"Abbie, once bail has been denied, there's nothing we can do except hope for a speedy trial and a light sentence," Ben put his hand on her arm and squeezed.

"What do you mean, sentence? I'm innocent!" Abbie couldn't help the moan that broke free as she crumbled into a heap on her cot. She pulled her knees up under herself in a yoga-like child pose and buried her face in the pillow. It stilled smelled rancid and Conrad was checking to see if he could bring her one from home. It would be one little comfort. Surely they wouldn't deny her that. She threw it across the cell and Ben caught it mid-air.

"Abbie, you've got to pull yourself together. If we're going to stick with the plea of innocence, then we've got to look at every piece of evidence they have and you have to help me come up with an argument that will provide reasonable doubt. You have no alibi since you were undeniably seen at both scenes." He set the pillow back on the cot.

Abbie sat up. Her shoulders sagged. "Sounds pretty grim but I'm telling the truth."

"Well, the prosecution has already offered a plea bargain so they're obviously not 100 percent confident they'll get a murder conviction," Ben offered helpfully. "I guess they're not as confident as we first thought."

"Murder? Jesus, even though I heard them say it yesterday, it's still so hard to believe they think I killed anyone. I didn't. Please, you've got to believe me."

"Abbie, even if I believe you, we still have to convince a jury. Did you hear what I said though? There's a plea bargain on the table."

"What does that mean?"

"It means if you accept it, in other words, plead guilty to a lesser charge, then you wouldn't have to go through a lengthy trial."

"What are they proposing?"

"I don't know for sure. We have to meet with the county prosecutor later this morning and she'll tell us what she has in mind."

"You mean that she-devil who convinced the judge not to give me bail?"

"That's the one," Ben chuckled. "A real piece of work, isn't she? But, she's good at what she does Abbie. We really need to be on our game if this goes to trial. It'll be interesting to hear what she has in mind. She'll be here in a couple hours so let's hold off any preparation until then. I'll come back to get you," Ben motioned for the guard to let him out. "See you soon."

"I'll wait right here," Abbie grimaced, not liking the sound of her own attempt at sarcasm.

BEN RETURNED EXACTLY two hours later and escorted Abbie to the interview room where the prosecutor and an assistant district attorney waited for them.

"Hello ladies," Ben shook both their hands and pulled a chair out for Abbie.

"Ben, how are you?"

"We're fine Kate, except that my client seems to be remanded into custody since you didn't trust she would show up for trial, even though her husband is a cop on your very own police force," Ben busied himself removing a few files from his briefcase.

"Well, if your client hadn't bolted after killing her lover, even though her *husband* is a cop, we wouldn't be in this predicament now would we?"

Abbie squirmed and opened her mouth to retort. Ben put his hand over hers and slowly shook his head.

"Okay Kate, tell us what type of a plea bargain you have for us."

"It's a good deal and I strongly urge you to take it. We have your client in both places and directly connected to both victims. The evidence is rock solid."

"So you think, but from where I sit, it's circumstantial," argued Ben. "So what do you have in mind?"

"Involuntary manslaughter on both counts and five years for each; sentences to run consecutively," Kate began. "She'll be eligible for parole after six."

"Six years? In prison? No. I told you I'm innocent."

Ben looked at Abbie. "Are you sure?"

"I'm more sure about this than I've ever been of anything in my life," Abbie held Ben's gaze with a piercing intensity.

"Well, you heard my client... Sorry, no deal."

"You have advised your client that if she loses she could get a life with no chance of parole, haven't you?"

"I didn't kill anyone," Abbie sat up and stated defiantly.

Ben shrugged. "You heard her . . . no deal."

"Fine then. I guess we'll see you in court," Kate snapped as she packed up her files and marched out.

Ben didn't say anything more until the door had closed firmly behind them. He let his breath out in a long whistle.

"Okay, let's get started then. You know Abbie, we may have no choice but to put you on the stand. I need to hear everything so I can prepare you for the grilling you could get from this prosecutor. We can use this room as long as we need it." Ben pulled out his yellow legal pad, ready to take notes.

Abbie winced and started to shake her head. Ben held up his hand. "I'm not saying you will but we still need to be ready. She's tough and she won't let up on you so you've got to brace yourself. We've got some time since they'll present their case and their witnesses first. I'll do everything I can to avoid it but if you have to testify I need you ready. In the end, it's up to you to keep it together. Regardless, I have to know everything. Don't leave one little detail out."

Abbie took a deep breath and started at the beginning. She told Ben everything from meeting Joan at Rachel's and working together at the run to the intimate conversations, even about her hormonal mood swings, irrational thoughts and borderline depression. She recollected for him the night she ran into Joan's husband, who she thought was a flasher.

"It was self-defense," she said weakly. "It was slippery and I fell into him. I didn't know he hit his head."

"Sounds like a bit of an overreaction to me. Why didn't you just run to the nearest house?"

"I don't know. I just saw red. You weren't there. I thought he might attack me."

"Well, the DA wasn't there either and she's going to go for the jugular. If we're going to make a self-defense plea work, we'll need to prove you didn't know him, hadn't planned to meet him and weren't having an affair with Joan. As for Joan, they have your fingerprints all over the motel room, including the bathroom. The good news is that if there were any fingerprints on the hair dryer, they were obscured after it sat in the water for a time. I'm waiting for the coroner's report and I'm hoping the time of death was long after you left."

Abbie rubbed her eyes and dragged the last of the mascara she had been wearing in court the day before across her cheek. She looked at the black smudges on her knuckles and groaned. She thought about the tiny sink in her cell and wished like hell for a shower.

"Let's take a bit of a break, shall we? I've got my associate working on some background for us so we'll continue later this afternoon. Have something to eat and try to get some rest."

"Sure," Abbie thought about the soggy Sloppy Joe they fed her the night before and her stomach heaved. "Can you bring me some Tums, please?"

By around 4 o'clock Ben was back. After choking down a lunch of franks and beans that had chunks of fat, accompanied by a slice of white bread with a couple of spots of mold, Abbie had tried desperately to get some sleep but only tossed and turned, realizing just how dire her situation was.

"Do you think we have any hope of winning?" Abbie asked.

"Well, we're going to have a battle on our hands, there's no doubt about that. Let me run something by you. After what you said this morning about the symptoms you've been suffering I did some research. I found out that some women suffer such extreme pre-menopausal symptoms that it can lead to violent mood swings, bouts of depression, severe heart palpitations and even nervous breakdowns."

"So?" Abbie wasn't sure what Ben was getting at.

"So, maybe you should consider changing your plea to not guilty by reason of temporary insanity, maybe get a lighter sentence. Get you some help. We can bring in expert testimony to say you didn't know what you were doing."

"Absolutely not. I agree that I'm having a rough time with this change, but not so much that I would intentionally kill anyone. I told you, it was self-defense with Mark and I didn't kill Joan!"

Abbie was getting agitated and could feel her skin prickling with heat as the hot flash overtook her body. Ben watched as her face flushed a beet red and the beads of sweat broke out under her eyes and pooled in the crevice at the base of her throat. He handed her a glass of water as she fanned herself with the notepad that had been sitting in front of him.

"Have I just been witness to a typical hot flash?" asked Ben incredulously.

"Oh, that one was pretty mild," answered Abbie, still fanning herself. The crimson on her face slowly faded to pink and then back to her natural skin color. "I guess your wife is still too young to be going through this yet?"

"I guess so. She's in her early 40s," Ben calculated in his head. "Forty-three, I believe."

"Well, brace yourself. It could start any time now," Abbie gave him a sympathetic look.

"Is there anything I can get you? Oh, here's your antacid."

"No, I'll be alright, thanks."

"Isn't there some type of medication you can take? For the menopause stuff, I mean."

"Now, don't you start on me too."

Ben shook his head. "If I was going through something like that and there was a pill I could take to fix it, I would."

"I don't like taking pills and there are some serious side effects."

"Worse than this?" Ben waved his arm in an arc taking in Abbie's jail cell.

"I told you. One has nothing to do with the other."

"So, if you weren't depressed about going through this change and having extreme mood swings and feeling irritable, with the shifting happening to your body, you would still have been looking for some type of relief, out partying in the middle of the night, without your husband, taking drugs and hanging in a seedy part of town?"

"Maybe not. But I'm still not insane and I'm not changing my plea."

"Fair enough but maybe we'll use it to show that your judgment was somewhat off. Okay, for the time being, let's go over how you met Joan again. I need every single detail about any time you were with her."

Ben grilled Abbie for the next four hours that afternoon and almost every day after until the trial began. He gave her a break only during the three days it took to select the jury. Ben was pleased with the members of the jury that he and the prosecutor had finally agreed on, who were meant to be a jury of Abbie's 'peers'. It was made up of mostly women who were over 40, but racially mixed. He was hoping it would be a sympathetic group.

Conrad came every day and brought the boys by a couple of times. Abbie desperately missed them but didn't feel comfortable with them seeing her in jail.

"Guys, you really don't have to come in here. I know it's not a very pleasant place," said Abbie after their second visit.

"I know we don't have to, we want to," Trevor reassured her, handing over the Big Mac with fries she had asked him to bring.

"Yeah, what else would we be doing anyways... watching TV and playing video games?" Winston added. "Besides, we have to make sure you're eating properly." Winston smirked.

"That's really sweet but I'd rather you didn't see me like this," Abbie insisted. Not only did she think it was best for them not to be there but it was also so humiliating for her. "Please, Conrad," she looked beseechingly at her husband, "Don't bring them again."

After much cajoling, Abbie was finally able to convince them that they had better things to do—jobs, girlfriends, graduation—oh cripes! She had almost forgotten about that . . . blocked it from her mind. She had missed their graduation. Her eyes started filling with tears. She choked them back, not wanting them to see her cry. She was sure they had taken loads of photos but they weren't allowed to bring a camera into the jail and, it wasn't the same as being there anyways.

"I'll call you every day and give you all the blow by blow details," she promised. "And, it'll be over before you know it and I'll be home and in your business again. Then you'll be sorry," she said and wagged her finger at them.

They all avoided the fact that there was a distinct possibility that by the time the trial was over, Winston and Trevor would have started university and would be away. They were both planning to live on campus.

Well, she would cross that emotional hurdle when she came to it. She called to the guard that her visitors were leaving, gave them each a kiss and ushered them out of her cell, just like she always shooed them out of the kitchen while she was cooking. She could feel a wave of anxiety overtaking her and her stomach rising in her throat but fought it down until they disappeared through the outside door, then promptly vomited in the sink next to her cot. She reached over for the bottle of Tums Ben had brought. She had already put quite a dent in it. As she crunched down on the chalky, strawberry-flavored tablets, she hoped they would settle her stomach but knew it would most likely be a while before she'd be able to get her digestive system back to its semi-normal state.

CHAPTER 14

Abbie was led out of the jailhouse into a cool, clear morning and on any other day, she would have inhaled a deep lungful of the fresh air and smiled up at the sun, ready for a new day. A butterfly flew across her path, which under normal circumstances would have made her smile. She had heard that a butterfly crossing your path was good luck but she couldn't think of any reason to smile today; and the butterfly was mostly black so did that negate the good luck part? She wasn't feeling particularly lucky that morning and her stomach still hurt and her bowel was in spasms. It was day one of the trial and Abbie was bracing herself for the shit storm.

Conrad had made a good decision choosing Ben Hurst as her defense attorney. Not only was he well known and well respected in town but he was the perfect balance between kind and supportive and strict and disciplined. He reminded her of some of the boys' favorite teachers over the years, demanding, but fair. He had been tough on her but she knew it would be a different feeling altogether if she wound up having to take the stand and someone who wasn't on her side asked the same questions and she wasn't prepared. Ben had assured her that they were ready for trial but she still said a little prayer as she and the young rookie driving the police car covered the short distance to the courthouse.

Abbie entered the courtroom wearing the same blue suit that she had worn at the arraignment. It was the only one she had. Ben said it was important to look serious and conservative. Conrad had promised to go out and buy her another one for the next day and have the blue one dry-cleaned. She couldn't believe she was worried about the damn suit when she was looking at the possibility of going to prison for murder. But Ben said it was important to look strait laced and motherly.

She gave herself a mental shake as the policeman took the cuffs off and she sat down next to Ben, folding her hands on the table in front of her. Ben covered her hands with his and she felt the reassuring scratch of the calluses. She always trusted someone more if they knew how to work with their hands. It was a nice combination along with his training and success as a criminal attorney. She made a mental note to ask him, when this was all over, what he did that gave him those roughened hands. She relaxed ever so slightly trying to bring her shoulders down from around her ears.

"All rise. The Honorable Judge Courtney Rayburn presiding."

"You may be seated. Counselors, are we ready to start?" Judge Rayburn inquired.

I guess there's no easing into this, Abbie thought. *Here we go.*

Ben rose again. "The defense is ready, Your Honor."

"The prosecution is as well, Your Honor."

"Okay, Ms. Masters, your opening statement please."

"Thank you Your Honor," Kate Masters was a statuesque woman and Abbie guessed she had to be close to six feet tall.

She had noticed when Kate and Ben had stood side by side in the interview room that she was almost as tall as him. She wore a tailored black, pinstriped pants suit with a simple string of pearls and matching earrings. She strode purposefully towards the jury box and put her hands on the rail.

"Ladies and gentlemen of the jury, what we have here are two clear-cut cases of cold-blooded murder. The defendant, Abigail Slocum, was having a lesbian love affair with one of the victims, Joan Bezanson. We will show you how the relationship grew over a short, yet intense, period of time. Witnesses will testify seeing them together in nightclubs and restaurants on several occasions. We will prove that when Joan's estranged and distraught husband, Mark Waller, confronted Ms. Slocum and told her he wanted to reconcile with his wife and threatened to tell her husband, Ms. Slocum, in a jealous rage, smashed his skull in with a rock. Then, after a booze and drug-filled night out partying with Ms. Bezanson, she realized she wanted her marriage to work and, not wanting her husband to find out, brutally killed Ms. Bezanson by electrocuting her in the tub of a sleazy motel room in which they had spent the night together. We will prove beyond a reasonable doubt that Ms. Slocum had the means, the motive and the opportunity to commit both of these heinous crimes. Thank you."

Ben stopped writing on his yellow legal pad, slowly put down his pen as he watched the DA swagger confidently back to her seat. He stood up to his full, broad, six-foot-three height, straightened his tie, cleared his throat and approached the jury box. "What the prosecution has told you just now would make a great crime novel but the fact is, it's just that—fiction. My client is a loving wife and mother who has been experiencing a slight emotional upheaval over the past few months but sought solace among a couple of female friends, one of whom was Joan Bezanson. Joan's death was a terrible shock to everyone, including my client. The death of Mark Waller, Ms. Bezanson's soon to be ex-husband, was an accident. We will show that the circumstances surrounding his death were not as sordid as the prosecution has fabricated, but a simple case of mistaken identity and, ultimately, self-defense. We will prove that Mr. Waller was in the neighborhood, looking for my client's home but she was unaware of this and had no idea who he was when she happened upon him that night. Thinking he was a flasher, she defended herself against what she perceived was a threat to her personal safety. I hope you will weigh all the facts and not allow yourselves to be duped by the circumstantial, smoke and mirror drama that the prosecution will play out here to convince you that their concocted version of the story is true. Thank you, ladies and gentlemen, for your time." Ben scanned across the jury box, making eye contact with each and every member of the jury, acknowledging their presence and almost thanking them individually. They were already nodding. Abbie thought that must be a good sign.

"Alright Ms. Masters, you may call your first witness."

"The prosecution calls county coroner Bruce Platt."

The coroner looked about a hundred years old to Abbie but that probably meant he had tons of experience and would be a rock solid witness.

"Please state your name and position for the record," the court's clerk said robotically, holding the bible ready for the witness to swear his oath.

"Bruce Platt, New Bedford County coroner."

"Please put your right hand on the bible. Do you swear to tell the truth, the whole truth and nothing but the truth, so help you God?"

"I will."

"You may be seated."

"Your witness Ms. Masters."

"Thank you Your Honor." Kate turned towards the witness box, pushed her glasses higher up on her nose and folded her arms. "Mr. Platt, can you please share with the jury how long you've been working for the state of Massachusetts?"

"Going on 30 years."

"And, how long with the New Bedford County prosecutor's office?"

"Almost 25."

"And, in that time, how many autopsies have you performed?"

"I've lost count by now but it's in the thousands for sure."

"Your Honor," Ben interrupted. "We know the witness has extensive experience in his field, can we please move on?"

"Duly noted Mr. Hurst. Ms. Masters, please get on with the relevant questioning."

"Thank you Your Honor. I will."

Ms. Masters picked up a file from the parallel stacks on her desk. "Mr. Platt, can you please tell us the cause of Mr. Waller's death?"

"Yes, it was blunt force trauma to the back of his head."

"So, could the injury that resulted in his death have been caused by someone hitting him on the head with a rock?"

"Objection your honor, leading the witness."

"Objection sustained Mr. Hurst. Ms. Masters please rephrase the question."

"Yes, your honor." Kate inclined her head slightly in acknowledgement, paused and turned back to her witness.

"Mr. Platt, in your opinion, what could have caused the injury that ultimately led to the death of Mr. Waller.

"The wound is consistent with a round, hard object that was most likely a rock."

"And, was there a rock found at the scene with Mr. Waller's blood on it?"

"Yes, there was."

"Can you tell us what the time of death was?"

"I put the time of death somewhere between midnight and two a.m."

"And, would the assailant have to had been very strong?"

"As a matter of fact, the angle at which the wound was made and the location of the injury wouldn't have taken much force at all. It was in the softer tissue at the base of the skull."

"In your opinion, could the defendant have been his attacker?"

"Yes, in my opinion, it's possible."

"Were there any other signs of a struggle?"

"Yes, the deceased's eyes were reddened by what we determined was a significant amount of capsaicin, more commonly known as pepper spray."

"And, as for the death of Joan Bezanson, did you determine the cause of death in that case?"

"Yes, I did. She was electrocuted by a hair dryer while sitting in a bathtub filled with water."

"And, the time of death?"

"Sometime between seven a.m. and nine a.m."

"Thank you. No further questions." The DA walked slowly back to her seat and fixed Abbie with a stare that made her shudder and shrink deeper into her chair.

"Defense, your witness."

"Thank you Your Honor." Ben's eye narrowed as he glanced over at the witness, looked briefly at his notes and rubbed his hand across his chin before he began.

"Mr. Platt, you've testified that it's possible that Mark Waller's injuries could have been caused by someone hitting him on the head with a rock. Is that correct?"

"Yes, that's correct."

"Isn't it equally as possible that the deceased fell over backwards and hit his head on the rock, thereby causing his death?"

"Yes, that's possible too."

Ben checked his notes again and rubbed the back of his neck.

"You also shared with the court that Ms. Bezanson's time of death was sometime between seven a.m. and nine a.m."

"Yes, that's correct."

"We have a witness that saw Ms. Slocum leaving the hotel just shortly before seven. Isn't it possible that Ms. Bezanson died after my client left that hotel room?"

"Yes, it's possible."

"It most certainly is. I thank you sir for clarifying that." Ben scanned the jury, nodded his head and raised his eyebrows, then turned to the judge. I have no further questions for this witness."

He sat back down next to Abbie and gave her a thumbs-up under the table. Abbie wasn't adept at reading the nuances of a jury like Ben was and still thought they looked skeptical, staring at her like she had 'murderer' tattooed across her forehead. Or, maybe it was just the paranoia seeping into her subconscious again.

"Ms. Masters, please call your next witness." Judge Rayburn's voice broke into Abbie's reverie.

"Thank you Your Honor. The prosecution calls Detective Jacob Stanley."

Abbie closed her eyes as the detective, one of Conrad's co-workers, was sworn in and took the stand. She didn't turn around but could hear the creak of the wooden bench behind her as Conrad shifted his position. She could sense his discomfort like a cold draft wafting around her neck and settling heavily on her shoulders. How could she have been so stupid? She felt a horrible sense of guilt. Her heart constricted and seemed to skip a beat as she thought about what she was putting her family through. She opened her eyes and turned her attention back to the witness stand as Jacob was answering the prosecutor.

"Yes, I was the first detective on the scene for both victims," he acknowledged her question.

"Please describe the scene for us when you found Mr. Waller, the first victim."

"When we arrived, the victim was already dead and had been for a while. It was obvious he had a fatal head injury. He was partially obscured by a hedge which is why he wasn't found until late the next morning."

"Did you find anything that would have caused the injury?"

"Yes, there was a rock sitting close to the body that was covered in blood. The body was at the bottom of a slight incline and it looked as though it had rolled away from it. The coroner confirmed that it was his blood on the rock."

"Could someone have purposely rolled the body into the bushes to conceal it?"

"Objection Your Honor," Ben stood up, placing his hands solidly on the defense table. "Calls for speculation."

"Your Honor, Detective Stanley is an experienced crime scene detective and his assumptions would be based on hard evidence or previous experience."

"I'll allow it. Detective, you may answer the question."

Ben sat down, his eyes narrowed in concentration ready to catch his adversary in any potential mis-step. Abbie watched the unspoken sparring between the two and would have been even more fascinated if her life wasn't the punching bag being hammered in between.

"There was no sign that would indicate that anyone purposely moved the body," the detective answered testily. "It was pretty muddy and there was a spot right at the top of the incline that showed that a struggle may have taken place but the closest foot print was three or four feet from there and it was facing in the opposite direction."

"Yes, the footprints," Kate walked over to her table and pulled a set of 8x10 photos from a file, glanced at the jury and walked up to the judge's bench. "Your honor I'd like to submit as evidence photos of the footprints Detective Stanley has referenced."

"So submitted," the judge acknowledged.

"Detective Stanley, during your investigation, did you determine what size shoe made these prints?"

"Yes."

Kate cocked her head and crossed her arms impatiently. "And, what size was that, detective?"

"They appeared to be made from a ladies size 8."

The prosecutor glanced towards Abbie and slightly inclined her head. The detective followed her glance and quickly dropped his gaze to his hands that were gripped in his lap. Abbie felt bad for him. It was probably uncomfortable for him testifying in a case against a fellow cop's wife. The clichéd scenario in the movies that the brotherhood among policemen was practically thicker than blood was true in real life. She had seen it time and time again in their own circle of friends who were mostly Conrad's brethren.

"And the scene at the hotel where Ms. Bezanson was discovered— please describe that for us."

"She was in the bathtub and it was full of water and there was a hairdryer in the bathtub with her. The hairdryer was plugged in."

"Like someone had dropped it in on purpose?"

"Objection, your Honor. She's not only leading the witness but this also calls for speculation."

"Objection sustained."

"No further questions." Kate nodded towards the jury, shrugged her shoulders and returned to her seat.

"Your witness Mr. Hurst."

"Thank you Your Honor. Detective Stanley, was there any sign of a struggle at the hotel?"

"No, not that I could tell."

"And, was there a shelf close enough that the hair dryer could have been sitting on and accidentally fallen into the tub?"

"Yes, there was."

"And were there any finger prints found on the hairdryer?"

"Yes, but it had been sitting in the water for a while so they were only partial prints."

"Did any of them match my client's?"

"No they did not." Jacob seemed almost relieved to have been asked the question and able to answer in the negative.

"Thank you detective. No further questions."

"Re-direct Your Honor?" Kate called from her chair.

"Go ahead counselor."

"Detective Stanley, did you find the defendants prints elsewhere in the motel room and in the bathroom?"

"Yes."

"Thank you. Nothing further, Your Honor."

"You may step down Detective Stanley," the judge motioned to him and then checked her watch. "Looks like it's time for a break. The court will take a short recess for lunch and will re-convene at two p.m. sharp. Court adjourned."

THE REST of the afternoon was a blur as Abbie tried desperately to keep her emotions in check. After lunch, the prosecution continued with their witnesses.

"The prosecution calls Brian Scully to the stand."

Abbie squinted at the witness, trying to place his face.

"Can you please tell us where you work Mr. Scully?"

"I'm a bouncer at *The Orchard*," he shifted slightly to get more comfortable in the small witness box, which looked even smaller filled with his bulky frame. Abbie didn't really recognize him but that was probably because she was already drunk when they had gotten to *The Orchard*.

"And can you tell us what your relationship to Joan Bezanson was?"

"She was a regular at the bar. I used to see her at least once, sometimes twice a week."

"Did you see her the night she died?"

"Yes, it was the weekend and she always came on the weekend."

"And, do you see anyone in the courtroom today who might have been with Ms. Bezanson that night."

"Yeah, two people."

"Please point them out."

"The lady in the first row there with the yellow blouse," he pointed to Rachel, "and the blonde woman right there," he pointed towards Abbie.

"Let the record show that the witness has pointed towards the defendant."

Kate paused and let that information sink in with the jury.

"You have a great memory... you must see hundreds of people every weekend."

"Yeah, but I know our regulars and make it a point of watching who they come in with. Joanie's on, I mean was on, our regulars list... you know... the ones we let jump the line." He puffed out his chest to show his importance, his already tight shirt pushing at the buttons. "She and her girls were looking pretty hot that night and were well-lubed." He winked at Abbie. She squirmed and re-crossed her legs under the table turning slightly sideways towards Ben.

"What do you mean 'well-lubed'?"

"They were obviously drunk."

"Okay, go on."

"Well, Joanie always brought a different woman so it sort of became a game with the bouncers and bar tenders."

"What kind of game?"

"Uh, we had a running bet on whether or not she would leave with the same woman she arrived with." He looked at Abbie again and she felt a hot flush suffuse her face and wished she could slap the smug look off his face. She stole a glance at Ben and could see he was seething and chomping at the bit to have a go at this guy.

"Did you notice anything else?"

"Yeah. They were pretty cozy too. Holding hands and everything."

"So you saw them throughout the night as well?"

"Sure. The bathroom's just inside the door so I get a clear view of that too. I saw Joan and blondie here going into the bathroom a couple of times and they always came out hugging or holding hands and definitely high on something."

"So, they looked like they were more than just friends?"

"Objection Your Honor!" Ben's jaw flexed as he clenched his teeth.

"Overruled. Mr. Scully, you may answer the question."

"Yes ma'am. They looked like friends with benefits, if you know what I mean." He smirked at the DA.

"Mr. Scully, yes or no would be sufficient thank you." Judge Rayburn scowled at him. "Please continue Ms. Masters."

"Thank you Your Honor. Mr. Scully, what makes you think they were high?"

"I've seen the look hundreds of times. I know the difference between just being drunk and being high. They were flyin'."

"Thank you Mr. Scully. No further questions."

"Your witness, Mr. Hurst," Judge Rayburn motioned to Ben.

"Thank you, Your Honor," Ben scanned his notes. "Mr. Scully, do you have a record?" Ben quickly scanned the jury as he asked his question and saw eyebrows raise and a few jurors leaned forward. Just the reaction he was hoping for.

"Objection, Your Honor, this witness is not on trial," Kate stood up and shot Ben a look.

"Your Honor, it goes to credibility," Ben had expected the objection. He stood up, walked towards the witness and cast a confident look toward the judge before locking eyes with 'Brian the bouncer'.

"I'll allow it, but make your point and move on Mr. Hurst."

"I will," Ben approached Brian. "Please answer the question, Mr. Scully. Do you have a record?"

"Yes, I have a record," Brian cracked his knuckles.

"Can you tell us what for?"

"Assault. It's a hazard of the profession."

"And, is there anything else about the charges? Something about a hate crime?"

"They dropped those charges," Brian glared at Ben; his hands were balled up in fists.

"But wasn't the man you assaulted gay?"

"I don't know... maybe."

"Would you call yourself homophobic?"

"Objection!" Kate jumped from her seat.

"Sustained. Mr. Hurst, please keep your questions relevant to the case at hand."

"Your Honor, it is relevant. If this witness is homophobic it's very likely that he's over-playing what he saw between my client and Ms. Bezanson that night."

"He saw what he saw Mr. Hurst," Judge Rayburn replied. "The jury will disregard defense counsel's last question."

"Okay, no further questions, Your Honor.

"Very well. You can step down Mr. Scully." The bouncer extricated himself from the witness box, shot Ben a look and then smirked at Abbie as he passed by her. Abbie shuddered. *What a jerk. And, Joan thought he was her friend.*

The Prosecution called their next witness. Abbie winced as she heard Joan's friend Simon's name being called. She knew how close he and Joan were and felt bad for him. She didn't think she'd be able to look him in the eye.

"Please state your name for the record."

"Simon Brady." he was so nervous it came out as a whisper.

"A little louder so the jury can hear please."

"Simon Brady," he said a little louder.

Simon was sworn in and took his place in the witness box. He smoothed his hands over the front of a perfectly pressed mauve collared shirt, tucked into a pair of tailored, black pleated pants. He nervously pushed thick black-rimmed glasses firmly onto the bridge of his nose and folded his hands in his lap.

He sure looks different from when I met him. Good thing he's not in drag. This is already enough of a circus. Abbie fidgeted in her seat while her knee bobbed uncontrollably under the table. Ben reached over and put his hand on her knee to calm her down.

She listened as the prosecutor grilled Simon about the night at *The Orchard.* Simon's testimony confirmed what they already knew and testified that yes, Joan was gay and that the girls had been drinking heavily all evening; and then he added another nail to Abbie's coffin.

"Mr. Brady, I know you've just lost a very dear friend and that this is difficult for you so just take your time." In a flare of sympathy, Kate handed him a Kleenex and waited as Simon wiped his eyes and took a drink of water.

"You've heard testimony from the bouncer that he thought that Joan and the defendant were high. Did you witness them doing any drugs?"

"Yes, we all went into the bathroom and Joan had some Ecstasy. She gave me one and then they both went into a stall together." Simon choked back a sob.

"Okay Mr. Brady, take your time." Tears were flowing freely down Abbie's face as she listened, some for Simon and some for herself as she listened to his recollections from that night. Abbie didn't remember him coming into the bathroom with them.

"What did you hear Mr. Brady?" The DA prodded.

"I didn't stay very long after—you know—three's a crowd. But I heard them giggling and then I heard Abbie say that it felt good." He shot Abbie a furtive look and then beseechingly back at Kate, begging her with his eyes to stop the questioning.

Abbie grit her teeth and worried how Conrad was taking it. Simon also confirmed that he saw Abbie leave with Joan shortly after one a.m.

"I have no further questions for this witness." Kate sat down and crossed her arms and swung her chair sideways to face Ben and Abbie, as if in victory, and then swung back to face the judge.

For the first time Abbie thought things might not go in her favor. Ben stood up, approached Simon and leaned on the witness box like he was conspiring.

"This was the first time you had met Abbie, wasn't it?"

"Yes, that's correct."

"And how did you know the victim?"

"She was a regular at *Rick's Place*, a bar I work at," Simon looked down at his hands. "We'd gotten to know each other pretty well and hung out a lot after I finished my shift."

"And what do you do at this bar?"

"I'm a performer."

"What type of performer are you?"

"Objection, Your Honor. Relevance?"

"I'll show relevance in just a minute Your Honor."

"I'll allow it. Objection overruled. Please answer the question Mr. Brady."

"I'm a headliner in the drag show."

"And, are the clientele at *Rick's Place* mostly gay and lesbian?"

"Yes, and transgender."

"How often would you say Ms. Bezanson was there?"

"Oh, I couldn't count. She'd been coming regularly, almost every weekend, for about six months now."

"So, how well would you say you knew her?"

"I knew her really well. We often went out dancing after I finished my show at *Ricks*." Simon's voice caught in his throat.

"And was Ms. Bezanson happy?"

"Sometimes yes and sometimes no. She was really moody."

"Why was that?"

"Well, she had recently 'come out' and left her husband and she still wasn't too sure she'd done the right thing. Her husband was calling her constantly and begging her to come back. Said they'd work it out."

"But she was sure she was gay?"

"She was pretty sure. And she tested her theory just about every weekend."

"And had she told you anything about my client before you met her that night?"

"She said she had met this woman through a friend from her singles group and she really liked her."

"Did she tell you this woman's name?"

"Yes. She said it was Abbie."

"What else did she say?"

"She said she knew Abbie was straight but she was going to do her best to work on that."

"Did Ms. Bezanson have any serious girlfriends that you know of?"

"No, she was pretty much playing the field but when she first started coming around she and Jami Wilson, our bartender, really hit it off for a while."

"So, they were pretty serious?"

"More serious on Jami's part, I think. Joan was still sorting it all out."

"And was Ms. Wilson working the night my client came into *Rick's* with Ms. Bezanson?"

"Yes, she was. They all sat and talked for a while until the show started. Jami was trying her best to get Joan's attention but Joan was all about Abbie and I could tell Jami wasn't very pleased about it either."

"Thank you Mr. Brady. I have no further questions."

"You may step down, Mr. Brady. Ms. Masters, please call your next witness.

"The prosecution calls Peter Riley."

"Your Honor, the defense doesn't have this name on the witness list," Ben, flipped through his files, irritated at the curve he was being thrown.

"Your Honor, my associate just found this witness this morning. And, if I can also note, this is a hostile witness."

"So noted. Mr. Hurst, you'll have your chance to question the witness. Ms. Masters, you may proceed."

The clerk swore in the witness. Abbie thought he looked like he had slept in his crinkled suit. He had at least a few days' worth of stubble on his face and what looked like toothpaste smudged on his chin. He was somehow familiar to her and she wondered where she would have seen him before. He reminded her a little bit of that TV detective who had died— Peter Falk—Columbo! *Oh jeez, is he the guy who Winston pointed out taking pictures at the run?* Abbie wondered. She also remembered seeing him outside the wine bar that same day.

"Mr. Riley I know you'd rather not be here but I will remind you that you're under oath. Can you please state your name and occupation for the record?" Kate began her questioning.

"Peter Riley and I am a private investigator."

"Can you please tell us what your relationship with the deceased, Mr. Waller, was?"

"He was a client."

"And, what did he hire you to do?"

"I was following his wife."

"That would be the other victim, Joan Bezanson, correct?"

"Yes, that's correct."

"And, when was the last time you saw your client?"

"The day before he died."

"What was Mr. Waller's frame of mind at the time?"

"Objection, Your Honor. Calls for speculation," Ben gripped the side of the table trying to maintain his composure. Abbie could tell his wheels were turning, thinking about how he would address this surprise witness.

"Objection sustained. Please rephrase the question Ms. Masters."

"Mr. Riley, was your client upset when you last saw him?"

"Yes."

"How could you tell?"

"Well, it was hard not to. You don't need to be a shrink to know when someone's pissed off. He was chain-smoking and pacing and yelling."

"Why was he so upset?"

"Because his wife was leaving him and he was still in love with her. He knew she was having an affair and wanted to know who it was."

"So, did you find out?"

"I only saw her with women so when he confronted her she admitted she was a lesbian."

"And, this made him mad?"

"Yes."

"Did you have photos of his wife with other women?"

"Yes."

"Was the defendant one of these women?"

"Yes."

"Were they incriminating photos?"

"No, not compared to some. You see a lot in my line of work and sometimes it's not very pretty. But, I did have a few choice ones that would make your imagination go wild."

"Did Mr. Waller's imagination go wild?"

"You could say that."

"Did you give him Ms. Slocum's address?"

"I didn't want to but he was very convincing."

"Did he say he was going to confront her?"

"He didn't say," Riley started to bite his fingernails and shifted his position. "He just wanted to see where she lived. He assured me he wouldn't do anything rash."

"No further questions, Your Honor."

"Mr. Hurst, your witness."

"Thank you." Ben flipped through a random file, stalling for time, gathering his thoughts. "Mr. Riley, did you ever see my client and Ms. Bezanson interacting in a romantic way?"

"It depends on what you think is romantic."

"Mr. Riley, you know how women are. They're different from us guys. They hug and hold hands and kiss when they greet each other."

"Yeah, I guess so."

"So, did you see them doing anything more than what you would see best girlfriends doing?"

"Probably not."

"Where were the pictures that you had of the two of them together taken?"

"Two places… a charity run and in a wine bar."

"And, in both places, weren't there other people with Ms. Slocum and Ms. Bezanson."

"Yes."

"In one instance Ms. Slocum's son was even there. So, you couldn't really consider it a clandestine rendezvous between two people sneaking around having an affair, could you?"

"No."

"During your surveillance of Ms. Bezanson, were there other women you saw her with and did you capture them in more intimate, maybe more compromising circumstances?"

"Yes."

"Can you tell us the woman's name?"

"Her name was Jami. She was a bartender at *Rick's Place*."

"And, did you give Mr. Waller her address too?"

"Yes."

"Thank you Mr. Riley. No further questions Your Honor."

"Mr. Riley, you're free to go."

"Ms. Masters, do you have any more witnesses to call?"

"No, Your Honor. The prosecution rests."

"Okay, we'll wrap it up for today. Mr. Hurst, we'll start tomorrow with your first witness. Court adjourned until nine a.m."

The sound of the gavel felt like it was landing on Abbie's last, frayed nerve. She jumped and her heart started pounding.

"I think that went well today," Ben turned to face her and squeezed her shoulder. Abbie wasn't so sure.

He turned to Conrad and shook his hand. "I'm glad you're here. I'm sure this is tough for you but it's important that the jury sees you're supporting Abbie."

"Of course I'm supporting her. Where else would I be?"

Abbie leaned over and he gathered her into his arms. It was the first time he had held her since that first day in jail. It felt good.

"Ma'am, it's time to go," her young police escort took her arm and gently crossed it behind her back. She let go of Conrad and put her other arm behind her back so that he could put the handcuffs on her.

"Is that really necessary?" Conrad questioned the rookie, who he had seen around the station but didn't really know. There were so many new young guys since a slew of the old guard had recently retired, Conrad couldn't keep track of them all.

"I'm sorry sir, it's required procedure," he shrugged apologetically.

"I know... you're just doing your job. Sorry. Abbie, I dropped the other suit off at the jailhouse so you'll have it in the morning. Get some rest and I'll see you tomorrow."

"Tell the boys I miss them," Abbie said.

"Don't worry, I will. They miss you too."

"Abbie, I'll meet you at the jail in half an hour. We have some prep work to do for tomorrow," Ben packed up his briefcase. Shook Conrad's hand again. "We're going to beat this. I can feel it. I think we've just got a break. I have to return a call to one of my associates so I'll keep you posted. Hopefully it's good news."

"Thanks Ben."

"Yeah. Sure thing." Ben practically ran out of the courtroom.

"Let's go Mrs. Slocum." The rookie gave her a gentle tug.

ABBIE FIDGETED in her cell while she waited for Ben to arrive. He had sounded pretty excited about something and she was anxious to find out what. She didn't feel nearly as confident as Ben but she told herself that he knew best.

As hard as she tried, she still couldn't remember what had happened in the motel room and that was the biggest strike against her. In her mind, she re-traced every step she took and everywhere they went that day but it got real hazy once they left *Rick's Place*. She had vague memories of dancing at *The Orchard*, of Simon arriving in drag (that was hard to forget), of taking the pink pill in the bathroom with Joan, the disco ball and flashing lights, the crush of bodies on the dance floor and then the recollections went blank. But, even if she did remember, it would just be her word against the evidence.

She heard the far door open and close and Ben's assertive stride coming down the corridor. The guard let him in and closed the cell door behind him.

"What's the crazy grin all about," Abbie asked as Ben pulled the chair over to the cot.

"Sit down Abbie, I have some great news," Ben was like a schoolgirl, bursting to tell her some gossip.

"Okay, I'm sitting. What's got you so jazzed?"

"Well, remember this afternoon when Simon was on the stand and he was talking about Jami the bartender and then the P.I. brought her up again?"

"Yes, I remember," Abbie was puzzled.

"Well, I had a hunch and so I texted my associate, Janice, to get a photo of her . . . the bar had one in her personnel file. I thought I would test out a crazy theory, although after what Simon said, and after what I found out, I know now that it wasn't so crazy after all."

"Ben, you're not making any sense."

"Sorry. I just did a mental leap and assumed you were there with me," he smiled at her. "Abbie, Janice took the photo and showed it to the motel manager and, guess what?"

"Jeez Ben, just tell me!"

"He recognized her and said she came into the motel after you left. She walked in like she owned the place so he didn't pay much attention and didn't see which room she was going to. He didn't see when she left either but we can put her at the scene after you left and closer to the time of death."

"So, what does that mean for me?"

"Abbie . . . Jami was the jealous lover scorned," Ben said patiently. "She came after you left. We can easily shift the jury's attention from you to her and create plenty of reasonable doubt."

Abbie picked at her skirt and tears of relief started rolling down her face.

"Don't worry. We're going to win this. But, it's not over yet. I just wanted to come by and tell you the good news. I've got a long night ahead of me so I've got to go. Tomorrow we have Rachel and Jami on the stand. I'm hoping we don't have to put you on as well but it'll depend on how it goes. There's a kid down the street who says he saw the whole thing with you and Mark. I've got to read the police report again to make sure he's not going to trip us up somehow. I think it's solid though. He can verify that you were surprised when Mark stepped out from behind the hedges and that it didn't look like a planned meeting. He can also corroborate your story that you didn't crack him on the head with a rock."

"I didn't see anyone but that's great. How did you find him?"

"He told his mom what he had seen after watching a report on the news about the trial and she brought him in to the police station. A lucky break for us." Abbie nodded. "Okay, I've gotta go but I'll see you first thing in the morning. Hopefully with this good news, you'll sleep like a baby tonight."

"Yeah sure," Abbie sighed and closed her eyes as the guard let Ben out. She imagined Conrad trying to maintain a little normalcy for the boys. Tonight would usually be family movie night and she hoped they were watching a comedy. They usually watched an action film with the inevitable car chase or building blowing up. Once in a while they let Abbie pick the movie and she tried to shy away from anything they would consider a 'chick flick.' She actually liked their selection of movies and had a secret, serious crush on Steven Seagal and Dwayne Johnson, aka 'The Rock'. She had never admitted it because they would have teased her relentlessly. Abbie drifted off to sleep, still fully clothed, dreaming of rappelling down the side of a mountain strapped to Sylvester Stallone.

CHAPTER 15

When Abbie arrived the next morning the courtroom was packed. There wasn't much to do in a small town like New Bedford and word had gotten around that there was a titillating trial underway so it had become the entertainment of the decade. There wasn't an empty seat to be found.

Abbie recognized some faces but for the most part it was a sea of unfamiliar, unfriendly, scowling, accusing faces. The glares were like shots of dental Novocain that first felt like hooked needles driving into her but then left behind a feeling of numbness. They didn't know her. Why should she care? But, she did and she knew once the numbness wore off, she would feel bruised and battered. It wouldn't help Conrad in his dream to make detective either. With the recent spate of retirements there were several slots open and Conrad was one of the best candidates but there was competition from other precincts and from out of state. Being in the same precinct should bring his application somewhere close to the top and she prayed that her situation wouldn't hurt his chances. *He wasn't responsible. They would see that, right?*

She tried to shake it off as she sat down and turned towards Rachel and Conrad sitting behind her. She attempted a weak smile. They both smiled and took her hands in theirs and squeezed. Then Abbie saw something that made her blood run cold. *No...it couldn't be. The look that they just gave each other.* Abbie gave herself another shake. Her best friend and her husband? She had been spending way too much time alone in her cell lately and had been reading too many bad romance novels. She needed to focus and not let her imagination run wild. *They are just supporting each other through a difficult time. Jeez! I never used to be so paranoid. What the hell's the matter with me?*

Ben was busy unpacking his briefcase. He finally had more files stacked up on the table than the prosecutor. Somehow, that made Abbie feel more secure. She knew it was irrational. She didn't know, or care, what was in them, just that it was all in support of her defense.

Across the aisle Kate Masters, the master of gloom and doom (as Abbie had nicknamed her) and her sidekick were already seated, quite poised and waiting expectantly. *How do you exude such self-confidence?* Abbie wondered.

"All rise," again the booming voice of the clerk interrupted Abbie's daydreaming and she stood up and faced the judge. "The Honorable Judge Courtney Rayburn presiding."

"You may be seated." Judge Rayburn smoothed down her robe, sat down and tucked a stray hair back into the bun on the back of her head. Abbie wished she would wear her hair down at least one day. It really would make her more human. But, that wasn't her role. Her role was to lead the proceedings, maintain an objective demeanor and ensure that all sides were heard fair and square. And, she could do that whether her hair was up or down.

For the first time Abbie saw some gray coursing through

the dark of the Judge's hair. Maybe she was older than Abbie had first thought. Hopefully those years had given her an empathetic edge and not hardened her too much. Abbie wondered what it was like to be a judge. She imagined it wouldn't be very easy. She didn't envy Judge Rayburn's position but sure as hell hoped that Ben could win her, and the jury, over. Objectivity should still have a heart and if they just opened theirs Abbie hoped that they would see she was innocent.

"Defense, please call your first witness." Judge Rayburn started the day's proceedings.

"Yes, Your Honor. The defense calls Rachel Moore."

Rachel excused herself as she exited the front bench and pushed open the swinging gate that opened between the defense and the prosecution tables. The dividing line between the viewing gallery and the front of the courtroom was like the ropes around a boxing ring. Beyond that swinging gate was where all the action took place. Referees called the fight and fighters entered the ring with their fists encased in huge padded boxing gloves and mouth guards, some more effective than others. Some retreated battered and bloody and some came out victorious. Abbie closed her eyes, crossed her fingers under the table and prayed that her best friend would come out unscathed.

Rachel was sworn in and sat down in the witness box, twisting a used Kleenex around her fingers. Her eyes were red and Abbie realized with a tug on her heart, that Rachel had been crying. It didn't look like she had slept much either. Her usually carefree features looked pinched and worried. Her eyebrows came together in a sorrowful arch hovering over blood-shot eyes.

"Rachel, thank you for being here today," Ben began, with a sympathetic voice, meant to put Rachel at ease. "I know this has been really tough for you so I'll try and make this as easy for you as I can, okay?"

"Okay," Rachel's voice was surprisingly strong and clear. Abbie was a little relieved.

"How long have you and Abigail Slocum been friends?"

"Abbie and I met in college so we've known each other for about 25 years."

"So, would you say you're pretty close?"

"We've been like sisters to each other ever since we met," Rachel smiled over at Abbie.

"And, I would imagine you've spent a lot of time with Ms. Slocum and her family?"

"Oh yes. Our kids grew up together. Actually, mine are younger but her boys were just like big brothers to my girls and even babysat them. We've travelled together over the years too. I love her family like I love my own."

"Is Ms. Slocum gay?"

"No, she isn't."

"And, have you ever known her to experiment with drugs?"

"Oh God no. Abbie's as strait laced as they come. We partied a little in college but what kid doesn't? Once she got married she settled right down and started having a family. She waited until she was in her late 20s, until she met the right guy. She had been working as an administrator in a non-profit, working with at-risk youth. That's how she met Conrad. He was the center's police liaison. They were perfect for each other. They share the same values and are both really family-oriented. Abbie quit working after the boys were born. She didn't want anyone else raising her kids. I really admire her for that."

"And, have you ever known her to be violent?"

"Absolutely not. She's as gentle as a kitten."

"And, can you tell us how Ms. Slocum and Ms. Bezanson met?"

"I introduced them."

"Can you tell us the circumstances of the first meeting?"

"Yes, we were all volunteering at a charity run for breast cancer research and the day before the run, both Abbie and Joan came to my place to help put together packages for the runners."

"Have you known Ms. Slocum to do a lot of charity work?"

"Absolutely. Abbie's got a heart as big as all outdoors. After the boys started school she needed to keep busy but still wanted to be there for them when they got home from school. She's always got a cause or charity she's working with. She inspired me years ago to give back and that's how I started coordinating volunteers for the run."

"Thank you Ms. Moore. No further questions Your Honor."

"Ms. Masters, your witness."

"Thank you, Your Honor." Kate Masters sauntered up to the witness stand just a little too cocky for Abbie's liking. She wondered what she had up her sleeve.

"Ms. Moore, you were close friends with the deceased, Ms. Bezanson, correct?"

"Yes, that's correct. We met at a singles support group several months ago. We had both recently separated from our husbands."

"You've told us that you brought Ms. Bezanson and Ms. Slocum together to work on an event with you, is that correct?"

"That's correct."

"But you said that Ms. Slocum wasn't gay. Why did you introduce them?"

"I wasn't introducing them to set them up if that's what

you're getting at. Abbie's happily married. Unlike some people, I don't think of individuals as gay or straight, Ms. Masters, I make friends based on other things we have in common. I really liked Joan and knew that we'd all get along."

"And the three of you went out together on several occasions?"

"Yes."

"Did you notice any flirting going on between them?"

"Objection, Your Honor," Ben interjected. "That's a very ambiguous term."

"Objection sustained. Next question Ms. Masters."

"Were you with them the night Ms. Bezanson died?

"Yes."

"Did you see them doing drugs?"

"No I did not."

Abbie was relieved that Rachel was able to answer that question honestly as she was sure that they had been in the bathroom without Rachel when Joan took the drugs out.

"Would you say that your best friend, who you've known for 25 years, was acting differently than she normally does?"

"A little, yes. But, she wasn't used to drinking so much."

"Or doing drugs?"

"Like I said, I didn't see her doing drugs."

"But you did notice that she was acting strange?"

"I guess so, yes."

"Did you see them leaving together?"

"No. I was getting tired so I left before they did."

"So, you left your best friend, who was acting very strange compared to her normal behavior, behind in a night club with a woman she barely knew?"

"Yes, and I wish I hadn't."

"Hmmm . . . hindsight is 20/20, isn't it Ms. Moore? So you say your friend is as gentle as a kitten?"

"That's right. Abbie wouldn't hurt a fly," Rachel leaned

forward with her hands clenched around the railing of the witness box, emphasizing her point.

"What about the dog?"

"What?"

"The dog. Her neighbor's pit bull. Didn't she brutally kill it with a frying pan?"

"Objection Your Honor," Ben jumped up from his seat. "What has that got to do with this trial?"

"Your Honor, the defense witness brought up the fact that Ms. Slocum is as gentle as a kitten. We have evidence to the contrary."

"I'll allow it."

"Your Honor, could we have a brief recess so I can confer with my client. This is new to us," Ben looked over at Abbie and scowled.

"Take 15 minutes counselor."

"So, do you want to tell me what happened with the dog?" Ben was clearly upset. "I'm trying to paint you as a kind wife and mother who wouldn't hurt a fly. A frying pan?"

"I didn't think to tell you. I hadn't even thought about it since the morning it happened." Abbie told Ben the whole story up to the point where she told Winston to call the Animal Control Department at the police station. "When I didn't hear anything more, I thought it was over and done with."

"Well, somehow the prosecution got wind of it and got hold of the report."

"I'm so sorry but it really was an isolated incident."

"Yeah, that and Mark and Joan. Abbie, we can only hope that I can soften it a bit on re-direct and our other witnesses can turn it back around. Or, I may have to put you on the stand and ask you about some of your peri-menopausal symptoms and how it sometimes can cloud your judgment."

"No. I'd really rather not. One has nothing to do with another. Granted, my out of control hormones probably made me make some really stupid moves and admittedly left me in some unfortunate situations but you have to believe me, if I hadn't done what I did that dog would have ripped me apart. He'd done it before and was supposed to be chained. I was scared. He should have been put down. People weren't letting their kids out to play for the longest time."

"Okay, I won't push it for now. Is there anything else I need to know?

"No."

"Okay then, let's get back."

"ARE WE READY TO RESUME, Mr. Hurst?"

"Yes, thank you Your Honor."

"Okay, Ms. Masters, please proceed."

"So, Ms. Moore, did Ms. Slocum tell you about the dog."

"Yes, she did and she was distraught about it."

"Well, according to the report we have here Ms. Slocum wasn't there when Animal Control arrived. She hit the poor thing with a skillet, left it for dead and then ran off. And, left her son to deal with it. That's pretty cold."

"Your Honor, does the prosecution have a question?" Ben shot out.

"Yes, I do Your Honor. Ms. Moore, I understand Ms. Slocum went to your house after the incident. Did she tell you why she left in such a hurry?"

"She wasn't thinking straight."

"And why is that?"

"She's been suffering with hot flashes and mood swings

lately. She came straight to my place after it happened and was shaking like a leaf."

"How long did she stay with you?"

"It was a while."

"How long would you say?"

"I don't really know."

"Take a guess," Kate insisted.

"Probably five or six hours. We were getting packets ready for the run . . . " Rachel's voice trailed off as she realized where the prosecutor was going with her line of questions.

"So, even after she collected her wits about her and told you the story, including the part where she left her son to clean up the mess, she still stayed with you and didn't go home?"

"I guess so," Rachel answered weakly.

"No further questions, Your Honor."

"Re-direct, please." Ben rose from his chair.

"Of course," the judge waved Ben towards Rachel.

"Rachel, had Abbie told you about this dog before?"

"Oh yes. He was notorious in the neighborhood. I even watched for him before I'd get out of my car at her place. He had attacked and seriously injured two other people before. I think he was supposed to be chained and muzzled. I believe the courts had given the owner one last chance. The dog shouldn't have been there in the first place. If it had been chained like it was supposed to be, Abbie wouldn't have been forced to do what she did."

"So, she was rightfully scared for her life when she was confronted by this animal who should have been tied up and muzzled by court order?"

"Yes."

"Nothing further Your Honor."

"Okay, Ms. Moore. You may step down."

Rachel averted her eyes as she passed by Abbie. She was understandably shaken and headed straight out of the courtroom. Abbie wished she could have given her a hug. She didn't do anything wrong. She just answered the questions she was asked. Abbie would find the first opportunity she could to reassure her friend but for now, she had to keep her own emotions in check.

Ben leaned over to whisper to her, "Don't worry. She'll be fine. She's tough."

Abbie didn't have time to answer when the judge interrupted, "Call your next witness, please."

"Your Honor, we call Jim MacKay."

Abbie turned towards the back of the courtroom as a young boy, probably close to Winston and Trevor's age, was escorted to the front. His eyes darted around the room, taking in the full gallery, the stern-looking judge at the front and the serious jury. His eyes finally came to rest on the hard, wooden witness box where he was about to be seated. He swallowed hard and put his hand on the bible. Sweat was pouring down the side of his face. He looked like he was choking as he tried to loosen his tie before he raised his right hand. Abbie felt bad for him but prayed that he could keep it together, sound credible and, most importantly, would support her version of the story.

"Do you swear to tell the truth, the whole truth and nothing but the truth, so help you God?"

"I do," Jim's voice squeaked out.

"Be seated."

"Mr. MacKay, please tell us what you saw on the night Mr. Waller died."

"Well, I saw a lady walking around the corner and a guy come out from the bushes."

"And, what time would that have been?"

"I know it was after midnight. Probably closer to one."

"What were you doing outside so late?"

"I was watching a movie and went out for some fresh air."

"It was raining that night, wasn't it?"

"Yes sir."

"Weren't you getting wet?"

"We have a little porch on the side of the house with an overhang. I was standing under that."

"When the woman came around the corner, was she surprised by the man coming out of the bushes?"

"Objection, leading the witness." Ms. Masters fists were in a bunch as she leaned into her objection.

"Objection sustained. Please rephrase your question Mr. Hurst."

"Okay, Your Honor. Jim, how did the woman react when she saw the man come out from the hedges?"

"It looked like she was surprised and she stepped back."

"From where you stood, did it look like they knew each other?"

"No sir."

"What happened next?"

"Well, the guy started to walk towards her and she backed up a bit. And then she took her hands out of her pockets and lunged after him. She had something in her hand. I think it was pepper spray."

"Did you see them engaged in any sort of conversation?"

"No sir. She sprayed him and then it seemed like she tripped and fell on top of him."

"She tripped?"

"Yes sir. Then she pushed herself off and ran away."

"Did you see the man get up?"

"No sir. I went back inside."

"And did you call the police to tell them what you saw?"

"Not for a couple of days."

"Why not? Didn't the police go to your house and the neighbor's the next day to ask if anyone had seen anything?"

"Yes."

"Why didn't you say anything then?"

Jim looked into the gallery. Abbie turned around to see where he was looking. A woman who must have been Jim's mother nodded at him and smiled. "I thought my mom would kill me. I'm not allowed to smoke so I went outside so she wouldn't smell it."

"So once you heard what had happened you told your mother you had seen something and she took you to the station and you made a statement. Is that correct?"

"Yes sir."

"Well Jim. You did the right thing. Thank you for coming forward. And, you really should quit smoking too."

"Yes sir," Jim looked like he would probably never have another puff as long as he lived. *He'll live longer that way.* Abbie smiled to herself thinking there just might be one positive outcome in all this drama.

As the judge called for the prosecutor to question the witness, poor Jim actually looked like he was going to vomit any minute.

"Hi Jim," said Ms. Masters trying to sound sweet but Abbie didn't think she quite pulled it off. She sounded more like the witch trying to get Snow White to bite into the apple. Abbie hoped Kate Masters' apple didn't have a razor blade in it. "How far away would you say you were from the defendant and the victim that night?"

"Uh, probably about a hundred feet or so."

"And, you say it was raining."

"Yes ma'am."

"And, it was the middle of the night?"

"Yes ma'am." Jim chewed on his lower lip.

Kate walked back to her table and made a grand gesture of looking at her notes. She turned around and half leaned, half sat on the edge of her table and crossed her arms.

"So, you couldn't really hear whether or not anything was being said?"

"No, but it happened so fast there wasn't time for any talking."

"Just answer the question please Jim. Could you or couldn't you hear what was being said?"

"No, I couldn't hear anything."

"And, just to clarify . . . you said you saw the defendant *lunge* towards the victim."

"Yes ma'am."

"And after the defendant ran away, you did not see the victim get up?"

"No ma'am." Jim's voice quivered and Abbie felt her heart twinge for the poor kid. "I went right back inside the house."

"No further questions."

"Re-direct, Your Honor?" Ben jumped up with his finger poised in the air.

"Go ahead counselor."

"Mr. MacKay. You said you thought my client had pepper spray in her hand. Is that correct?

"Yes."

"At any time during the altercation did you see her pick up a rock?"

"No sir."

"Are you sure? It would have been dark."

"I'm pretty sure. There was a street lamp close to where they were."

"Thank you. Nothing further Your Honor."

"You're excused Mr. MacKay." Judge Rayburn shuffled the papers in front of her, took her glasses off and looked up. "Well, I think that's enough for this week. Court is adjourned until Monday when we'll continue with the defense witness-es." She gathered her flowing black robe and lifted it just above her ankles as she stepped down from the dais.

Abbie, Ben and the rest of the courtroom stood up and watched as she exited into her chambers in one impressively fluid motion. Abbie turned towards Conrad, relieved to see he was actually still there.

"Can you bring Rachel by to see me tonight? I really need to make sure she's okay."

"Sure. Is there anything else I can bring you?" Conrad's eyes darted around the courtroom obviously uncomfortable in his position on the other side of the law.

"I'd really like to see the boys too." Abbie's eyes stung from holding back tears as she thought about her two sons. She reached out desperately for Conrad's hand.

"Aw hon, I don't know if that's such a great idea. I think you were right to keep them away." He shoved his hands deep into his pockets. Abbie's outstretched hand fell to her side.

"Please Conrad. They must be seeing stuff on TV and I'd really like to be able to show them I'm okay."

"Are you sure?"

"I'm not really sure, but I think I have to." Her brow furrowed, not entirely convinced it was a good idea after all.

"Actually, I think it would be good for her morale Conrad," Ben offered. "And, from what I hear, those boys are pretty well-grounded."

"Yeah, they are. Okay, you're right. I'll bring them by with Rachel. It'll be like old home week," Conrad tried to make light of the situation but the weight of the trial was etched deeply in his eyes and around the grooves of his mouth. Abbie hadn't noticed the wrinkles around his mouth before. She prayed that she'd be able to help him smooth out the crevices when this was all over.

CONRAD, Trevor, Winston and Rachel arrived in the early evening armed with a feast. Rachel came in first, as the cell wasn't big enough for all of them at once. Abbie knew that she was being treated just a little differently than other prisoners since Conrad was on the police force. She knew that they were bending the visiting rules by allowing several visitors at once and for them to be able to bring her food.

Rachel handed Abbie a huge spinach salad, topped with boiled eggs, bacon, tomatoes and lots of mozzarella cheese.

"Oh my God... I haven't had anything this healthy in ages! Thanks Rach," Abbie took the salad from Rachel, put it on the table and reached over to take her into a big bear hug.

"Good lord, you're going to smother me Abs," Rachel laughed.

"I'm so sorry to put you through this Rach." Abbie's voice was muffled in Rachel's neck. "Watching that horrible prosecutor lay into you like that today was so awful!"

"Ah... don't worry. It stung at first but I'm tough. I'll survive."

"You look like you haven't slept in days." Abbie brushed a strand of hair from Rachel's forehead.

"Jeez, you're one to talk. You look like shit too. Your roots are even starting to show."

"What a pair, huh? When this is all over, I owe you a day at the spa."

"Make it a week and you've got a deal." The girls interlocked their little fingers and pinky swore.

Rachel looked down at her hands as she twisted an already tattered tissue.

"Abbie, I need to ask you something . . . " Rachel's voice trailed off.

"You can ask me anything, you know that." Abbie took Rachel's hand and looked her in the eye. "We've been friends forever and you know me better than anyone else and it breaks my heart to put you through this. I'm so sorry about what happened to Joan. I know you were real close to her too."

"That's what I need to know." Rachel squirmed and looked over her shoulder and lowered her voice to a whisper. "Was there something going on between the two of you?" She pulled her hand away from Abbie's and ran her fingers nervously through her hair. "I've been going over and over that night in my mind and all the time we spent together and I can see what people are talking about but I can't believe I could be so naïve to have missed something like that." The words spilled from her like the rapid babbling of a brook.

Abbie pulled Rachel's hand back and held it tightly. "Honey, no! There wasn't anything 'going on'. I have to admit, I did like the attention and I was curious but I love Conrad and there's no one else that makes me as happy as he does. I just got caught up in the newness of it."

Abbie shook her head wondering about the series of events that had lead her and her best friend to these unpleasant circumstances. Over the years they had shared heart to heart talks on every issue under the sun and knew each other's deepest, darkest secrets. Never in a million years would either of them have guessed that one of their sessions would take place in a 10 x 10 jail cell. What she would give now to trade the cold, grey surroundings for a year's worth of class mom duties and soccer game car-pooling.

"Honestly, I just needed something to take my mind off the boys leaving, not to mention my raging hormones. And, our little diversions with Joan did the trick." Abbie's voice caught in her throat. "I let it get out of control and I'll never forgive myself. I would turn back time if I could."

Rachel let out a gust of a sigh and her shoulders hunched. Tears welled up in her eyes and huge drops spilled over onto her cheeks. She reached over and wrapped Abbie in a hug and clung on while great sobs wracked her body.

"I've been feeling so guilty," she whispered into Abbie's hair.

"Guilty? What for?" Abbie grabbed her by the shoulders and held her at arm's length.

"For a lot of things," Rachel wiped her tear-streaked cheeks. "First, for thinking you could have anything to do with Joan's death and then for introducing you two in the first place." She inhaled a shuttering breath of stale, tinny air. "It's my fault Joan's gone and you're in this mess."

"That's crazy. Put that thought right out of your head right now!" Abbie took hold of both her hands and squeezed. "There's no way you could have known this would happen. Absolutely nothing about this is your fault." Abbie reached up and took Rachel's face between her hands. "Now, promise me you'll banish those thoughts right now and focus on putting this behind us."

"Okay, I'll try." Rachel attempted a weak smile and ran her fingers under her eyes to wipe away her smudged mascara. "Now, you've got a couple of very handsome young men dying to get in here to see you so I'd better get going."

"Thanks Rachel. You're the best."

"I know."

They hugged again and Abbie clung to Rachel like she was her life raft on a sinking ship. She couldn't believe she had ever suspected that there was something going on between Rachel and Conrad. Rachel had always been fiercely loyal to Abbie and her family. Why would that ever change?

Rachel called down the hall to the guard that she was ready to leave. He sauntered toward the cell and unlocked the door. He locked it behind Rachel and escorted her back down the hallway and out to the waiting area where the boys were.

He returned minutes later with Trevor and Winston following close on his heels. He let them in and the cell door clanged shut behind them.

"This is creepy," Winston said and hugged his mom.

"I know, but I'm dealing with it," Abbie squeezed him back. "I just close my eyes and imagine I'm in the kitchen making a huge pot of spaghetti, which isn't difficult since I've been doing it for you guys forever. It was the first solid food you ate once I weaned you off the strained prunes." She reached over to tug on Trevor's sleeve.

"How's it going?" Trevor squeezed her hand. There wasn't enough space for them both to sit on the cot with her and Winston still had his arm protectively around her shoulder as Trevor stood at the foot of the bed shifting his weight from one foot to the other. "The TV and newspapers are going nuts with this. It's all we see or hear anymore."

"Really? I haven't seen any of the coverage. I think your dad is trying to protect me."

"It's pretty brutal," Trevor began, his eyes darted around the cell, his discomfort palpable.

Winston glared at him. "Trev, I don't think she needs to hear the gory details."

"It's okay guys. But, Winston's right. I don't really want to know what they're saying. I just want you guys to know that I love you and your father very much and that I'm okay. Just don't believe everything you hear. And, if you have any questions I'll tell you anything you need to know."

"We love you too. Uh . . . I do have one question." Trevor began and then paused and looked down at his hands.

"Anything honey," Abbie looked up at him and slightly nodded her head encouraging him to continue.

Trevor shifted uncomfortably and cleared his throat a couple of times. "Are you a lesbian?"

"Trevor!" Winston tightened his arm around her shoulder.

"It's okay Winston. I said you guys could ask me anything and I meant it." Abbie turned to Trevor. "No, Sweetie, I'm not a lesbian. I know that's what they're probably saying in the media but they're just sensationalizing this."

"So, you're not leaving Dad?" Winston asked.

"No. Not if he can forgive me for starting this shit storm." The boys both laughed nervously, as Abbie rarely swore.

"Oh God, all he talks about is how when you come home we'll be able to get back to normal," Trevor said. "And, how he's going to take the vacation time he's been building up and take you away somewhere warm so you can start getting better."

Abbie felt a flood of relief come over her. "I'm so glad to hear that."

"What does he mean, so you can start getting better? Are you sick or something?" Trevor asked as he bit a fingernail off and spit it out on the floor and kicked it with one of his size 12 sneakers that were habitually unlaced with the tongue hanging out.

"No, I'm not sick," Abbie began, not really knowing how to explain it, deciding not to chastise him this time for biting his nails. "You're going to trip over your laces if you don't tie them... " Abbie said instead. Trevor started to retort but caught himself and waited for her to go on. "You know I haven't been myself lately, right?"

Both boys nodded.

"Well, I'm experiencing something called peri-menopause . . . and in some women it can cause extreme hormonal imbalance and sometimes even depression," Abbie paused to gauge their reaction.

"Are you depressed?" Winston asked tentatively.

"I think I've had some bouts in the last year," Abbie admitted. "But I promise you I'm going to be okay, especially since I know you guys are here for me and supporting me."

"Sure we are," Winston said and Trevor nodded in agreement, his brows were knit together like two caterpillars going head to head.

"That means more to me than you can possibly know," Abbie reached around Trevor's waist and hugged both of them tightly. "Trev... you okay? Something's still bothering you, I can tell. You'll get a head ache if you keep bunching up your forehead like that." Abbie's attempt at humor fell like a thud on the cold cement floor as Trevor looked down at her with pain and confusion in his eyes.

"Come and sit with me. Talk to me okay?" She motioned for Winston to change places with his brother who was obviously distraught.

Trevor sat next to his mother and crossed his arms. She could tell he was desperately trying to maintain control. He was so much like his father. Winston quietly backed up to the corner of the cell and leaned against the wall.

"I'm listening."

"It's just . . . I mean . . . I don't know mom. Jesus, what happens if you're found guilty? What happens to us? Did you think about that when you were out partying with your friends?" Trevor's voice raised as a wave of anger seemed to overtake his emotions.

"Trevor!" Winston advanced on his brother but Abbie held up her hand. "Winston, leave him be. It's okay. He has every right to be mad," Abbie tried to keep her voice from quivering.

She turned to Trevor. "I'm sorry to put you through this but I promise I'll make it up to you."

"No . . . I'm sorry mom," Trevor mumbled. "I didn't mean it. But, how can we make plans now to go to university in the fall when you're sitting here in this hell hole?" He looked at her beseechingly, the pain and anger quickly dissipating into worry. Abbie felt her heart miss a beat.

She took a deep breath, willing herself to keep it together

just until they left. She had plenty of time when she was by herself to fall apart.

"Oh honey, it's really not so bad. I'm fine and you shouldn't be worried. Ben's a great lawyer and he's sure this is going to go in my favor. You have to keep moving forward with your plans. Knowing that you are makes it so much easier for me to get up and face each day."

She hated to see them go but could feel the last of her resolve melting away. "You guys better go so I can have something to eat and get some rest. We can talk about this more some other time, okay?"

"Sounds great, right Trev?" Winston pulled his brother up from the cot. "You know Mom, you've been so cooped up with us the last 17 years, it's no wonder you went a little crazy," Winston tried his best to lighten the mood. "We know you're going to beat this and that you love us and you'll be back home real soon. Hang in there, will ya? We need you." They both gathered her into a double bear hug.

"Now enjoy the rabbit food Rachel brought." They released her and Winston pushed the take out container towards her. "Next time we'll bring you some real food."

Trevor stood stiffly at the door with his back to her, waiting for the guard to let them out. Abbie knew she would have to work harder for his forgiveness.

AFTER THE BOYS left and Abbie had finished her salad she slid gingerly under the covers, trying to minimize the horrible creaking sound that emanated from the springs. It reminded her of the sound of the birds in the old Alfred Hitchcock movie that had given her nightmares for years. She tossed and turned while she wondered why Conrad hadn't come in. Each shift in position brought the eerie sound back, over and over again, triggering more fear and paranoia. Were he and Rachel together now? When would he visit again? He had decided to work the weekend to keep occupied and wanted the higher ups to know he was still focused on the job. So it might be a couple of days before Abbie saw him again. She desperately needed to make sure that what the boys said was true. Needed to know that he would forgive her. Needed to look into his eyes and see for herself. With tears rolling down her cheeks, Abbie finally drifted off to sleep.

CHAPTER 16

The days came and went in a blur and Abbie was having a hard time keeping track. There was no calendar in her cell and the watch she had with her wasn't the kind that had a date on it. She made a mental note to ask Conrad to bring her the sports watch he had given her last Christmas. She only wore it when they went on dive trips. She had very dainty wrists so she felt it looked too bulky to wear every day, even though that seemed to be the style these days. And, it had all kinds of great features, including the day, date and time.

Abbie shifted on her cot, trying to get comfortable. She wasn't tired so she sat up and propped her thin pillow against the wall, folded it in two and leaned against it. She hugged her knees to her chest and rocked side to side like she did in yoga class to loosen tight lower back muscles. She wondered if they would let Conrad bring a pair of her flannel pyjamas as well. It was starting to cool down at night and the cement blocks of the cell walls held the cold like a bum on a grate clutching a blanket.

She tried to remember all the witnesses who had testified so far. There seemed to be an unending parade of people in and out of the courtroom. Ben had done a great job lining up character witnesses; from one of the teachers the boys had the year she was class mother, to the executive director of a charity for which she had been volunteering for years. The prosecution was equally as cunning. She went through a mental list of the Master of Gloom and Doom's henchmen and remembered a litany of cops who were at one or both scenes, forensic experts, Jack from the wine bar, the clerk at the bus station and even Bess, her busybody neighbor. Ben had done a good job poking holes in Bess's credibility, effectively making her look like the nosy neighbor, Gladys Kravitz, on *Bewitched*. Abbie stifled a chuckle. Even sitting there by herself, she didn't think it was appropriate to be laughing, considering the gravity of her situation. If anyone heard her they would think she was nuts... they probably already did. A giggle escaped her lips then her throat caught in a bitter sob of loneliness and desperation. She drove her balled up fists into her eye sockets, rubbing away the tears that threatened and chastised herself. "Get a grip Abbie. You can't lose it now." After the words were out of her mouth she looked down the hallway to make sure no one heard her talking to herself. The stress of the trial was taking its toll on her and her family. She felt so helpless and ashamed but she would still do whatever she could to protect them.

Ben had wanted to put the boys on the stand. He felt that they were mature enough and were a perfect demonstration of what a great mother Abbie was. She ferociously vetoed the idea, wanting to keep them far away from the trial as long as she could. It had become such a circus, she didn't want them swarmed by media or bombarded with questions from nosy neighbors and the crowd of voyeurs that seemed to grow every day. As she continued her contemplation on the trial proceedings she tried to block out the moist, metallic, moldy smell of the four walls that closed in on her more and more every day.

She swore to herself that if she got out she would never again complain about the locker room scent of the boys' rooms or moan about having to live in a frat house. She'd take that any day over this.

Abbie slept in fits and starts, her night filled with dreams of Conrad, Trevor, Winston and her, sleeping in piles of sweat socks and jock straps that filled the space where a bed would be. They all had great big smiles on their faces though. Even Abbie.

AS SHE WAS LED into the courtroom the next morning, the butterflies in Abbie's stomach threatened to break through the muscle and flesh barrier to the outside world. Her system had been out of whack for weeks (even more so than before) but the fluttering had turned into frantic battering around the walls of her stomach and wouldn't let up. She wasn't sure why this morning was any worse. Probably because Jami's testimony could make or break the case. It could also determine whether or not Abbie herself would have to take the stand. She really hoped she didn't have to. And, she desperately hoped that her 'change of life' symptoms didn't have to be highlighted any more than they already had been. She felt like it was a flimsy defense and knew that the prosecutor would view her as a weak female and rip her to shreds.

She couldn't help but wonder, though, if she hadn't been suffering from those horrible night sweats and wild, irrational thoughts if, first of all, she wouldn't have been out walking in the wee hours of the morning and, secondly, she may not have reacted so aggressively when confronted by the man she thought was a flasher. If her insecurities had not been heightened with her hormones so out of balance, she probably wouldn't have been flattered by Joan's attention either and she more than likely wouldn't have taken the drugs and would have gone home with Rachel that night.

Oh, woulda, coulda, shoulda, right? It happened and look at the mess I'm in. And, Goddammit, if I could just remember what happened at the motel that night.

"Are you doing okay today?" Ben's question brought Abbie out of her self-scolding musings. He leaned over and whispered, "I'm pumped Abbie. We're going to turn a corner today for sure. Up until now I think the jury's kind of been on the fence. Kate's good and very convincing and they seem to sway like a school of fish in a confused current, depending on who's presenting the argument. They're just constantly nodding, except for that dour looking woman in the front." Abbie rolled her eyes. She knew exactly the one he was talking about. "I'm having a hard time reading them but if Jami's testimony goes as I plan, that jury will be planted firmly on our side."

"I hope you're right," Abbie gave Ben as confident a smile as she could muster. She turned around for some reassurance from Conrad and he winked and smiled at her. Now, that was a bit of the old Conrad coming out. She had had a good visit with the boys the night before. They were amazing. She and Conrad had definitely raised them right. She and Conrad had also had a heart to heart. Abbie knew they had a lot more to talk about but felt in her gut that they had made a good start.

Abbie smiled and winked back at Conrad. Her butterflies finally subsided as she brought back the feeling of being wrapped up in her boys' arms. It felt safe and secure. She was ready to face the day now, whatever it would bring.

"Mr. Hurst, please call your next witness," Judge Rayburn said, almost on cue.

"Your Honor, the defense calls Jami Wilson."

Jami came through the back of the courtroom. Abbie saw tattoos showing through the see-through sleeves of her silk blouse, which she hadn't noticed that night in the bar since Jami had been wearing long sleeves... that weren't see-through. It made Abbie recall Joan's intricate, and a little disturbing, tattoo and she studied Jami's more closely. She could only see Jami's right arm clearly, as she stood at the front and faced the back of the courtroom, hand on the bible to be sworn in. Abbie felt a jolt as the details sunk in. It was almost a carbon copy of Joan's, down to the horns on the top of the angel's head and the serpent gripped in her hand. The serpent ran a little longer and narrower since it was going down the length of Jami's arm but there was no denying the similarities.

Abbie grabbed Ben's arm as he went to stand up. "She has the identical tattoo on her arm that Joan had on the back of her neck," Abbie hissed in his ear. Ben's eyebrows rose ever so slightly and a small smile played around the corners of his mouth. He gave Abbie a slow nod, gathered his notes and stood up.

"Good morning Ms. Wilson. Thank you for being with us today." Jami glared at him. She'd had no choice as she had been subpoenaed to appear. "I know this must be very difficult for you. I understand you and Ms. Bezanson were very close."

"Yeah, we were friends."

"Well, Ms. Wilson, according to your co-worker, Simon, and your friend, Brian the bouncer at *The Orchard*, you were more than just friends. Can you tell us what the nature of the relationship was?"

Jami sat silently glowering at Ben.

"The witness will answer the question," Judge Rayburn leaned over and looked Jami in the eye.

"She was my lover," Jami almost whispered, looking straight at the judge. Her voice cracked.

"I'm sorry Ms. Wilson. Can you please speak up so the jury can hear?"

"We were lovers," she said through clenched teeth as she turned back to face Ben.

"Actually, you were her first lover after she came out of the closet and left her husband. Isn't that right?

"I don't know. Maybe."

"At the time of Ms. Bezanson's death, you were really ex-lovers, right? Isn't it true that she had broken up with you and was seeing other women."

"Yes, but we were still close and talking about getting back together." Jami's voice caught in her throat. She ran her finger under her nose as Judge Rayburn handed her a tissue.

"I'm sorry Ms. Wilson. Take a minute to compose yourself." Ben paused as Jami blew her nose. "So, I'm sure it made you mad that she flaunted the others in front of you?"

"No." Jami lifted her head slightly in defiance, crushing the used tissue in her balled up fist.

"When Ms. Bezanson, Joan, showed up at *Rick's Place* that night with two new female friends in tow, it must have really stung."

"She was always bringing new friends in. It was good for business. Didn't bother me at all. I get a cut of the door, so the more the merrier in my opinion."

"When they left to go *The Orchard* and didn't invite you, didn't that hurt?"

"No, I had to work close anyways."

"Ms. Wilson, how late does the bar stay open?"

"It's a cabaret so we're licensed to open until three a.m."

"And when you're responsible for closing, how long does it usually take?"

"Well, once all the patrons have left, maybe a couple of hours."

"Okay, so, last call, clearing out the last stragglers plus a couple of hours... would you say you left sometime after six a.m.?"

"I guess that would be about right. Maybe a bit later since we usually unwind a bit with a drink."

"And did you go straight home after that."

"Uh, yes I did."

"Would you like to think about your answer Ms. Wilson? I don't think you did go straight home. We have a witness that can identify you and says you arrived at the motel where Ms. Bezanson was found and it was shortly after Ms. Slocum left, somewhere around 7:00 a.m."

"Okay, so I did go," Jami wiped a tear that escaped down her cheek and paused to blow her nose again. "But when I got there... she was already dead."

"So, why didn't you call the police?"

"I was upset and wasn't thinking clearly."

"I think it's because she was alive when you got there."

Ben flipped through one of his files. "We also have Ms. Bezanson's cell phone records that show she made a call to you after the time the motel manager saw my client leave."

Jami turned pale and looked like she was going to be sick. "He must have mixed up the time."

"Not likely, but on top of his eye witness account, the coroner puts the time of death after the time that Ms. Bezanson made the call to you. How do you explain that?"

"I don't know! I swear she was dead when I got there. She must have doubled back," Jami glared at Abbie.

"You don't like Ms. Slocum, do you?"

"Not particularly. She played hard to get which made Joan want her even more," she flipped her long blond hair back over her shoulder.

"You know Ms. Slocum is married, right?"

"Yeah, Joan told me but she was determined to get her into bed. She got really upset that nothing had happened that night so she called me..." Jami trailed off.

"So, she called you to come and console her?"

"She did that all the time. I was the one she really wanted. She just wasn't ready to admit it."

"So, it was an early morning booty call?"

"Your Honor! Objection." Kate slammed her hand on her desk.

"Mr. Hurst, please stick to the questions," Judge Rayburn chastised.

"Yes, Your Honor. That was uncalled for and I apologize." Ben shook his head and turned back to Jami. "So, Ms. Wilson, the evidence would indicate that Ms. Bezanson was alive when you got there."

"Okay, yes, she was alive but it was an accident. She was going on and on about Abbie and how pissed off she was that she had finally gotten her into the motel room but the little priss just wanted to 'sleep it off' before going home to her *loving* husband."

Abbie felt the color drain from her own face with the realization that nothing did happen with Joan. She was so relieved she almost cried out. She covered her mouth to muffle the cry and tried to listen to the rest of what Jami was saying.

"I tried to make her feel better but she just pushed me away."

"And then what happened?"

"I didn't mean it! It was an accident," Jami wailed. "I went to slap her. It was just a reaction. I couldn't help it. She pushed me away. Said she changed her mind and wanted me to go away. She said she wanted to be alone. She always did that. She'd push me away and then call me back when the flavor of the night didn't work out. I was sick of it! I loved her. I went to slap her and my hand caught on the cord of the dryer and it pulled from the mount, switched on as it hit the corner of the counter and fell into the tub," Jami crumbled into hysterics. "I didn't mean it. Oh, Joan, I'm so sorry!"

"Your Honor, I don't have any more questions for this

witness," Ben stepped away from the witness box, leaving Jami shaking and sobbing behind him.

The gallery erupted into lively discourse, amazed at their good fortune to be witness to such a sordid tale. Abbie overheard one voyeur tell his friend that he wouldn't be surprised if they made a Hollywood True Stories episode out of this one. Although there was no one famous involved in the trial there was definitely plenty of drama. Abbie hoped that wouldn't happen and that it would all just go away. On the other hand, maybe Julia Roberts would play her part, Abbie contemplated.

"Order in the court please," Judge Rayburn slammed down her gavel. "In light of these new developments, I think we need to take a break. Bailiff, take the witness into custody please."

The gallery burst into a renewed cacophony of chatter, guessing at what could possibly happen next.

Ben sat down beside Abbie and put his arm around her shoulder and squeezed. "One more hurtle and we're home free," he said triumphantly.

"Order!" Judge Rayburn made another attempt to quiet the courtroom. "If the gallery can't behave, I will close these proceedings. Court adjourned until two p.m." She banged her gavel again and the rabble started filing out, murmuring amongst themselves. They had obviously toned it down a notch not wanting to miss the final chapter.

WHEN BEN JOINED Abbie and Conrad in the court's conference room shortly after, he brought in thick, tuna sandwiches on whole wheat for the three of them to eat over their working lunch.

"We need to keep our strength up 'cause we're on the home stretch," Ben said happily as he distributed the feast.

Conrad walked around the conference table and shook Ben's hand and gripped his other shoulder. It was the closest thing to a hug between two men without both of them wrapping their arms around each other. "I don't know how to thank you," Conrad's voice quivered. "You've managed this like a pro and never wavered. Thank you."

"Just doing my job and it's not over yet. We're clear of one murder charge, thanks to Jami for cracking, but we've got one more to attend to. Come on, let's eat and I'll take you through what I'm planning for this afternoon's entertainment."

"I don't know how much more excitement I can take," Abbie unwrapped her sandwich and wondered if she'd be able to get one bite past the lump that had been in her throat for days but she was ravenous and willing to try. "We don't have any more witnesses, do we?" She bit into her sandwich like she hadn't eaten in days. It was heavenly. The lump in her throat slowly eased up and she could finally swallow her food. What a relief. "You said if it went well with Jami I wouldn't have to take the stand."

"Well, that's what I want to talk to you about," Ben leaned back in his chair. "No, I don't think we need to put you on the stand just yet but I do want you to re-consider letting me bring in the medical expert who can talk about extreme peri-menopause."

"Aw Ben, I thought we had put that one to bed," Abbie put her sandwich down and looked pleadingly at him.

"Now hear me out," Ben could be very convincing. Abbie wasn't sure she wanted to be convinced but stayed quiet indicating he could continue. "Mark Waller still died as a direct result of your actions, right?"

"I guess so," Abbie agreed.

"He's right honey. What do you have in mind, Ben?"

Conrad pushed his sandwich aside and put his elbows on the table giving Ben his undivided attention.

"Well, I think Jim's testimony certainly supported your version of the story, even if Kate was able to shed a slight amount of doubt based on what he could or couldn't hear. What we haven't been able to prove is that you didn't know who he was. However, it was clear enough from where Jim was standing that he could see that you did not purposely bash Mark's head in with a rock. He definitely hit his head when he fell backwards. The problem is, the prosecution has described it like you tackled him. So, what I'm proposing is that the medical expert testify that your symptoms were extreme enough that at that moment, when you were fearful of being attacked, you reacted more severely than you would have otherwise."

Abbie and Conrad were silent as they both thought about what Ben was proposing.

"We'll still play on the self-defense element but I think this will give us the extra edge we need to clear you totally," Ben added.

"Abbie, honey, I think it's a good play on Ben's part. I know you're worried about how it will pan out but I don't think we have anything to lose and a lot to gain. It could mean the difference between an acquittal and a guilty verdict."

Conrad knew his way around the legal system and Abbie trusted him with all her heart, and Ben too. "Okay. If you think it's really going to make that much of a difference, let's do it."

"Great!"

"She's already here isn't she," Abbie looked at Ben suspiciously.

"Yes, she is, but I knew you'd see it my way," Ben happily bit into his sandwich.

THE PLAYERS WERE ALL BACK in position at two p.m. sharp as Judge Rayburn called the court back in session.

"Mr. Hurst, does the defense have any more witnesses for us?"

"Yes, Your Honor, the defense calls Dr. Lillian Hamilton.

Dr. Hamilton was sworn in and took the stand.

"Good afternoon Dr. Hamilton."

"Good afternoon."

"Can you please tell the court your full name and profession?"

"My name is Lillian Hamilton and I'm a licensed Obstetrician and Gynecologist as well as a Certified Menopause Practitioner."

"Can you explain what that means exactly?"

"Yes, of course. It means that I have attained an additional level of certification beyond my medical degree in obstetrics and gynecology and my patients are mostly women between the ages of 35 and 55 who are experiencing peri-menopause and menopause symptoms. I mostly specialize in treating extreme symptoms and hormonal imbalance."

"What kind of symptoms are normal and how do you know when it's become extreme?"

"Well, as we all know, peri-menopause and menopause are normal phases in every woman's life where she goes through changes in her body, just like everyone does during puberty. Each woman experiences symptoms a little differently depending on her own body's make-up, some environmental factors and, of course heredity, but most experience the common symptoms of night sweats, hot flashes, irritability, sometimes extremely heavy bleeding leading to anemia, insomnia, fatigue, slowed brain function, and mood swings. Mood swings are normal but what's not normal is for the fluctuations to become so extreme or erratic that they seriously affect your quality of life. Hormone level fluctuations can become so wide and happen too quickly, outside the range that the body can handle. That's when I would diagnose hormonal imbalance and recommend treatment."

"Thank you for explaining that Dr. Hamilton. And, how long have you been practicing?"

"I've been practicing medicine for 25 years and became a Certified Menopause Practitioner more than 10 years ago."

"And, in that time, how many women have you treated?"

"It's got to be thousands now."

"And of those thousands of women you've seen, what percentage would you say suffered from extreme peri-menopausal symptoms?"

"The majority have been in the bounds of normal so I would say maybe 15 percent. But, that number is probably low. Some women can be 'in denial' for years before recognizing that their physical symptoms are beyond normal limits. They tell themselves that it's just part of a woman's life cycle and women have been going through it for years and they need to 'buck up' so to speak."

"When a woman is in denial, can she also make irrational choices that would be outside of her normal character?"

"Absolutely."

"And could the mood swings caused by the hormonal imbalance and the long-term repression of those feelings cause her to unexpectedly overreact to certain stimulus?"

"Of course. Mood swings are abrupt fluctuations in mood and can catch one off-guard causing a drastic shift in one's emotional state. An extreme mood swing is an emotional reaction that is inappropriately intense in comparison to the particular cause or trigger. The hormone imbalances will also temporarily interrupt serotonin production which increases the likelihood of mood swings, unexplainable emotions, aggression, anxiety, paranoia, depression and other psychological issues during that time."

"So, when my client was faced with what she thought was imminent danger, her fight or flight mechanism could have gone into overdrive due to a hormone imbalance and pushed her into an aggressive fight mode, in her mind, purely for self-preservation?"

"Yes, that's quite likely."

"Thank you Dr. Hamilton. No further questions, Your Honor."

"Your witness, Ms. Masters," Judge Rayburn pushed her glasses up her nose and leaned towards the witness box, seemingly engrossed by the doctor's testimony.

Maybe she's been repressing something? Abbie looked at the judge with renewed interest. Could there be a chink in the armor? A little empathy, perhaps?

"Dr. Hamilton, you said that all women react differently to 'the change' didn't you?" Kate began.

"Yes, that's correct but there are a lot of commonalities as well."

"And, have you ever examined Ms. Slocum?"

"No, I have not."

"So, you don't really know just how severe her symptoms may or may not be?"

"Objection, Your Honor, Dr. Hamilton was called to testify about the generalities of the condition based on her years of expertise, not to specifically address my client's situation."

"Objection overruled. Dr. Hamilton, you may answer the question."

"No, I can't speak specifically to Ms. Slocum's symptoms."

"No further questions Your Honor."

"Thank you Dr. Hamilton, you may step down," Judge

Rayburn looked down at her notes. "Mr. Hurst, do you have any more witnesses?"

"May I have a moment to confer with my client, Your Honor?"

"Go ahead Mr. Hurst."

Ben leaned over and whispered in Abbie's ear, "I think you should take the stand Abbie."

"Oh God, why?"

"As good as Dr. Hamilton was, she really couldn't speak to your actual symptoms. You have to tell the jury what you've been dealing with. They have to hear it from you. If you don't they'll think you've got something to hide."

"But... "Abbie's voice trailed off. "Okay. If you think I should. But, just for the record, I'm not happy about it."

"Atta girl. Don't worry, it'll be fine," Ben patted her on the back.

"Your Honor, the defense calls Abigail Slocum to the stand."

Abbie rose from her seat and turned to look at Conrad. He raised his eyebrows in surprise and Abbie shrugged. She pulled down her suit jacket and smoothed it down, took a deep breath and walked to the witness box.

"Do you swear to tell the truth, the whole truth, and nothing but the truth, so help you God?"

"I do," Abbie responded.

"You may take the stand."

Abbie sat in the witness box and folded her hands on her lap and stared straight forward. She saw Conrad nod his head in encouragement and she unclenched her hands.

"Abbie, how are you holding up?" Ben was standing close with his hand on the railing of the witness box.

"Okay, I guess."

"I know this has been quite a horrible ordeal for you and

your family but you've been managing really well. So, take a deep breath and we'll get through this."

Abbie inhaled and exhaled and kept her gaze on Ben. She was scared to look at the jury. Ben had coached her to try to look into each of their eyes but she wasn't ready yet. She'd wait until he started asking his questions and until the churning in her stomach calmed down. She was petrified of the prosecutor and hoped she could remember everything Ben had told her to do in the event she had to take the stand. She had sort of put it out of her mind, thinking they were going to avoid it at all costs. She wondered if Ben had it planned all along. She felt he had kind of sprung it on her but she supposed that what clinched it was when Kate had asked Dr. Hamilton if she had examined Abbie and her answer was no. Now, she had no choice but to roll with it.

"Abbie, how long have you been experiencing symptoms of peri-menopause?"

"Let me see . . . I guess it's been almost a year now that I've really known what was going on."

"So, would you say they really started before that?"

"Yes, I suppose so."

"But, you were in denial?"

"Objection, Your Honor," Kate interrupted. "Mr. Hurst isn't a therapist and he's leading the witness."

"Sustained. Mr. Hurst, please re-phrase the question."

"Abbie, did you realize you were in peri-menopause?"

"I thought I was too young to be starting already."

"So, you were denying the possibility that it was happening to you?"

"That's probably true."

"Could you relate to any of the symptoms that Dr. Hamilton described?"

"Yes."

"Which ones?"

"All of them."

"Can you please describe what it feels like to have all these symptoms?"

"It felt like I was falling apart all at once, both mentally and physically. I had a family I had to take care of but everything they said or did was irritating me and it seemed like they were constantly criticizing everything I did," Abbie's voice caught in her throat and the tears welled up in her eyes.

"Take your time Abbie," Ben walked over to the defense table and poured a glass of water from a pitcher and brought it back to her. "Please, go on."

Abbie gratefully took a drink and handed the glass back to Ben. "I feel anxious all the time, my pulse races at the slightest thing. And, then there are the horrible night sweats that I've been having for a while. I have to change my nightie several times a night and wash the sheets practically every day. More recently I started having a hundred hot flashes a day. It's like you're coming to a slow boil from the inside out. People look at you strange because your face turns to bright red. Most times the anxiety and feelings of helplessness come along with it making it even worse."

"And what goes through your mind when you experience these frequent episodes?"

"That I'd be better off . . . my family would be better off without me. I'm such an emotional wreck." The tears were flowing freely down Abbie's face at this point and she avoided looking at Conrad, scared that he might think she was being weak and foolish.

"Abbie, I know this is difficult so just take your time," Ben stopped and put his hand over hers and looked into her eyes, almost transferring his strength into her. "Let us know if you need a break."

"No, I'm fine," Abbie blew her nose and sat up straighter.

She didn't want it to go on any longer than absolutely necessary.

"Okay. Now, you said you thought your family would be better off without you. What did you mean by that?"

Abbie took a deep, shuddering breath. "I just thought at one point that I could put us all out of our misery. A misery I was causing."

She looked over at the jury and was surprised to see that one woman in the front who, from day one, had been watching the proceedings with a steely, cold attitude was wiping her eyes. Finally, she stole a glance in Conrad's direction and he had tears rolling down his cheeks. Her heart ached for him. She wished she had talked to him about this before he heard about her feelings in an open court in front of all these strangers. He had been witness to the physical symptoms (they were hard to miss when you're lying next to a woman who's a sopping wet furnace) and had tried his best to help but he didn't know about her internal anguish. She should have trusted him.

"Did you talk to anyone about it?"

"Not really. I mentioned that I was having hot flashes to my doctor but that was all," Abbie went on, feeling like she was on display. "I didn't say anything about killing myself. It just felt silly talking about it. I never would have done it." She felt raw and vulnerable but knew there was no stopping now.

"And, what did he say?"

"He wanted to put me on anti-depressants."

"And, you didn't want that?"

"No. I don't like taking pills. I thought I could handle it."

"When you had more suicidal thoughts, did you go back?"

"No," Abbie's voice was barely audible.

"Do you think maybe your symptoms are a bit on the extreme side and maybe you could use some help dealing with them?" Ben asked quietly. The entire jury seemed to lean forward to hear her answer.

"Yes."

"No more questions, Your Honor."

"Ms. Slocum, do you feel like you can continue?" Judge Rayburn asked. Abbie thought she heard a hint of concern in her voice. "Would you like a break?"

"No Your Honor, I'm fine. I'd like to just continue, please," Abbie sniffed. She just wanted to get it over with and go back to the safety of the defendant's table next to Ben.

"Fair enough. Ms. Masters, your witness." Judge Rayburn sat back.

"Thank you." Kate walked up to Abbie and handed her a Kleenex. It was a kind gesture but Abbie wasn't about to let her guard down yet.

"Ms. Slocum, did you feel these waves of irritability and anxiety when you killed the dog with a frying pan and when you attacked Mr. Waller?" As Ben had anticipated, Kate went directly in for the kill.

"Yes I did."

"And, when you have these waves of irritability with your husband or children, have you ever used a frying pan or pepper spray to shut them up?"

"Of course not!" Abbie almost stood up. She wanted to wipe the self-satisfied smirk from her face.

"So, you still have control over your actions, even when you're experiencing one of these so-called episodes?"

"I guess so." Abbie looked beseechingly at Ben. He slowly dropped his head in a subtle nod, encouraging her to go on.

"Just yes or no, Ms. Slocum."

"Well, yes." Abbie gathered up the pieces of Kleenex on her lap, not realizing that she had been shredding it.

"And, you say you don't like taking pills?"

"That's right," she tried to sound defiant.

"But you didn't hesitate to take the drugs Ms. Bezanson offered you?"

"Objection," Ben interjected. "Your honor, there's no proof that my client took any drugs, only the assumptions of a witness whose credibility is questionable, not to mention the fact that the circumstances surrounding Ms. Bezanson's death are no longer at issue. So, this question is irrelevant."

"Objection sustained."

"I have no further questions Your Honor," Kate gave Abbie one last, penetrating look and turned and walked down the length of the jury box before returning to her seat. Abbie felt drained.

"Ms. Slocum, you may return to your seat," Judge Rayburn said softly to Abbie. "Mr. Hurst, do you have any more witnesses?" Judge Rayburn asked as she scanned her copy of the witness list.

"No Your Honor, the defense rests."

"Ms. Masters?"

"The prosecution rests as well, Ma'am."

"Very well. We'll re-convene tomorrow morning at 10 a.m. to hear closing arguments. Court adjourned."

Abbie rose, along with Ben, as Judge Rayburn exited to her chambers behind the dais. They watched the jury file out. "Do you think we've convinced them?"

"I think we made some great headway. You were brilliant. I'm sorry you had to go through that but at least we gave them something else to think about other than debating whether or not you had met Mark before that night. I think we're in good shape."

"I *didn't* know him and I had never met him before that night, so hopefully the truth will set me free," Abbie couldn't help giving Ben a lop-sided grin as she thought about Jim Carrey saying something similar to that at the end of her favorite movie, *Liar Liar*.

"Glad to see you still have your sense of humor."

She turned towards Conrad and he reached for her. She leaned over the railing and buried her face in his shoulder. "Abbie, I had no idea. Why didn't you tell me? We can work this out together. We always have."

She shrugged not wanting to let go. She inhaled his familiar scent and it infused her with a feeling of serenity. He held her tighter. "You did great. We're going to get through this, you'll see."

"I'm sorry ma'am but I have to take you back." The same young cop who had been there throughout the trial took her arm and gently led her away. If she wasn't so emotionally exhausted she might have actually felt a spring in her step, which she hadn't felt in a long time. She did finally feel that everything was really going to be okay.

CONRAD BROUGHT Trevor and Winston to visit that night and they begged her to allow them to attend the final arguments.

"Mom, we've stayed away all this time only because you insisted," Winston rationalized. "Now Dad says that you're going to have a positive outcome and we want to be there for you."

"Yeah Mom," Trevor chimed in. "Why wouldn't you want us to be there and witness the victory first hand?"

"They have a point Abbie," Conrad joined the chorus.

"But they'll be re-hashing all the evidence and there's stuff I'd rather they not hear," Abbie argued weakly. "And, we don't know what the outcome is going to be. It could still go sideways on me."

"Mom, you've got to think positive. And, besides, we've heard most of it on TV and Dad's filled us in on the rest,"

Winston took her hand and looked into her eyes, which he knew worked wonders on her.

Abbie glared at Conrad.

"What? You'd rather they heard it on the streets? You keep forgetting, they're men now. They can handle it." Conrad took her other hand as Trevor put his head on her shoulder and smiled up at her. The cell was pretty crowded with all of them there but Abbie didn't feel smothered... she felt protected and knew they just wanted what was best for her.

"Okay, okay. But if there's really nasty stuff you hear about your mother that you really would have preferred not to know, don't say I didn't warn you."

"We've heard it all Mom. Don't worry, we still love you and still think you're square," Trevor fake-winced as Abbie punched him on the shoulder.

"Come on guys, let's go and let your mom get some rest. We've all got a big day tomorrow."

"Bye Mom . . . give 'em hell! We'll see you tomorrow."

"Bye boys. I love you."

"Love you too, Mom."

The boys had left Abbie with a lingering warm, fuzzy feeling but Abbie still couldn't sleep. She tossed and turned as she kept having visions of Joan and Mark. No matter what, two people were dead and probably would still be alive if it hadn't been for her. Even though she had been exonerated for Joan's death, she still felt horribly guilty and sad. Sad for Joan; sad for Jami; and sad about the whole damn situation.

Even though Joan had sort of manipulated her, she would still hold a special place in Abbie's heart. In the short time they had known each other they had had a lot of fun and Joan had helped her break out of her funk. And, Abbie knew that Joan had been a good friend to Rachel too and had helped her through her rough time. This had been brutal for Rachel and Abbie knew she would have some mending to do. She knew her suspicions about Rachel and Conrad were just her active imagination. She'd been spending so much time lately with just the company of her own thoughts, which was dangerous. It was so easy to let her mind wander.

She also knew now that Joan had been struggling with her own emotional upheaval. She hid it well under a façade of blustery bravado but it was clear now that she hadn't been as grounded and comfortable in her skin as Abbie had thought.

Finally she drifted off to another dream-filled sleep interspersed with faces of friends and family, lively courtroom debates, judges banging gavels and juries line-dancing in the middle of a courthouse complete with disco balls and multi-colored lit-up flooring.

CHAPTER 17

As Abbie sat down at the defense table next to Ben she shared her psychedelic dreams from the night before. Ben laughed, "Sounds like my kind of courtroom."

Abbie took a deep breath and braced herself as Judge Rayburn entered the courtroom and began the proceedings. Abbie was surprised to see the judge's hair out of its bun and flowing down past her shoulders. It gave her a much softer look. Abbie wondered why the change.

"Is the prosecution ready to present its final summation?"

"We are Your Honor." Kate Masters was just as buttoned up and officious as the first day of the trial. She stood up, took a final look down at her notes, yanked her suit jacket down into place, walked towards the jury and began speaking.

"Ladies and gentlemen of the jury, thank you so much for being here. I know this case had been a very challenging one to hear. When there is not one but two victims, it can be unsettling. Especially when it's happened in your own back yard and when the victims have met such untimely and horrible deaths. That makes it even more chilling. The fact that the defendant has been cleared of Ms. Bezanson's death doesn't mean that she didn't have some responsibility for it. She still had a direct hand in the circumstances that led to her death. Although you will not be deliberating on that case anymore, I ask you to keep that fact in mind when deciding on her innocence or guilt in the death of Mark Waller. There is no doubt whatsoever that she was directly responsible for the death of Ms. Bezanson's husband. She was placed at the scene, aggressively attacking him and she then fled the scene after she killed him. Mr. Waller did have photos of his wife with Ms. Slocum, taken by his private investigator, Mr. Riley, and the defense would have you believe that he jumped to the wrong conclusion. Either way, he was still distraught and he still confronted Ms. Slocum with his suspicions upon which she attacked and killed him. She was scared that Mr. Waller would tell her husband. You've heard expert testimony from a doctor who specializes in extreme peri-menopause and menopause symptoms and the defense would like you believe that Ms. Slocum was not entirely in control of her actions the night she killed Mr. Waller. Ladies and gentlemen, at least half the population of this world is female and if we anticipate that half the population, upon reaching between 35 and 55 years of age, would have a built in excuse to overreact violently to every emotional whim, we would have anarchy in no time. I ask you not to send that message and to find Ms. Slocum, guilty of murder in the second degree. Thank you for your time.

Kate Masters looked every juror in the eye before slowly turning around and returning to her chair.

"Thank you Ms. Masters," Judge Rayburn seemed impressed with the prosecution's closing remarks. Abbie hoped she would be equally as impressed with Ben's. "Mr. Hurst. Whenever you're ready."

"Yes, Your Honor," Ben flashed his most winning smile at the judge and then swept a glance along the length of the jury box. Abbie knew that the jury couldn't help but notice his charisma. But, it was more than that. He was kind and warm and she knew that had come across during the trial as well and would bode well for his critical closing performance. Because, that's exactly what this was... a performance of the highest caliber actors, strutting their stuff on a legal stage, soliciting emotion and sympathy and presenting their hopeful alternative endings. Abbie knew full well that Ben and Kate were equally skilled. She had noticed the jury nodding a lot during the prosecution's summation. But as Ben had said, they seemed to sway in the direction of whoever was speaking. They were now in the final act of this play. However, the final scene was in the control of the elite in the box seats, the jury, who would pen the ultimate ending.

"Ladies and gentlemen of the jury," Ben began. "I would first like to thank you for your tireless commitment to this process and wish you luck in your deliberations. In my summation I will give you a little more insight into the character of my client, I will review with you the key evidence and also touch on the circumstantial evidence that should have no bearing on your decision. I will also illustrate why there is enough reasonable doubt and that there is only one logical conclusion to this case." Ben paused and looked over at Abbie and turned back to the jury. "Please take a minute to look at my client. Ask yourself if she looks like a mad, maniacal killer like the Prosecution has painted her out to be? No. She is a loving wife and mother, whose husband has been here every single day of the trial, supporting her. Today, her sons are here as well. They were not here before because she insisted that they not be exposed to the stress of the trial process. Like any mother, she is fiercely protective of them. She's a good mother. My client, Abbie Slocum, is also a community volunteer who has raised significant funds for her chosen charities, including one for breast cancer research. Abbie's mother died of breast cancer less than a year ago, which added to an already difficult time she was having and which directly impacted her decision not to take any type of hormone replacement therapy. Having a history of breast cancer in her family, combined with this type of treatment would increase the likelihood that she too would get breast cancer. My client has admittedly been experiencing some emotional issues relating to her peri-menopause, which could have influenced some of her decisions lately. She found herself in a set of unfortunate circumstances that led to the *accidental* death of Mr. Waller for which she is terribly sorry. Peter Riley, Mr. Waller's private investigator, indicated that Mr. Waller did not know my client so, when he surprised her that night and she pepper sprayed him, she was simply acting in self-defense. The prosecution has tried to lead you into the belief that my client and Mr. Waller had met before but there is no corroborating evidence to indicate that is the case. They have fabricated a sordid love triangle that simply didn't exist and, therefore, neither does my client's so-called motive for killing Mark Waller. She has been cleared of the death of Joan Bezanson so, even though my colleague has asked you to consider this death in your deliberations as to whether or not my client is guilty of murder, it is not appropriate, or fair, to do so. This element has been eliminated from the equation. Furthermore, Jim MacKay's sworn statement and subsequent testimony under oath in this court clearly showed that Abbie was surprised by a man who she thought was going to attack her. There was clearly no conversation between them. Mr. MacKay also testified that he did not see her hit Mr. Waller with a rock. She pepper sprayed him in self-defense. It was raining and slippery that night. She very likely lost her balance and fell into him. He fell backwards and accidentally hit his head on the rock, which caused the blunt trauma, which killed him. Ladies and gentlemen, in bringing my summation to a close I ask you this: If the meeting between my client and Mr. Waller was supposedly scheduled and she *was* planning to intentionally cause him harm, wouldn't she have been carrying something a little more lethal than just pepper spray? Being married to a policeman, she takes precautions when walking alone and normally, as a rule, carries the spray with her. There was no pre-meditation, no malice, no motive, no illegal activity and, therefore, no murder. Abbie Slocum has been a victim of unfortunate circumstances and has been living a nightmare for weeks... an innocent woman locked up in a jail cell, away from her loved ones and vilified on the local news. She feels saddened by the death of these two people and prays for their families but she should not be punished for being in the wrong place at the wrong time. Please help her end this nightmare and find her innocent. Thank you for your kind and patience attention."

Ben folded his hands in front of him and tilted his head, seemingly pondering his last statement. His eyes swept the length of the jury box twice before he slowly turned, walked back to the defendant's table and took his place again beside Abbie.

"Ms. Masters, do you have any final closing remarks?"

"No, Your Honor."

"Very well," Judge Rayburn turned to the jury box. "Ladies and gentlemen of the jury, the prosecution and defense have presented their respective cases and have offered their final arguments. You now have the responsibility of reviewing all of the evidence presented in this case, evaluating the arguments presented by both sides and rendering a verdict. The charge facing the defendant is murder in the second degree, which is a killing that is not premeditated or planned or committed in a reasonable heat of passion but where there is intent to cause the death of another person or there is reckless indifference to human life. If you are to consider a guilty verdict, make certain that you know for sure, *beyond a reasonable doubt*. Good luck with your deliberations. You may retire to the jury room until you have come to a unanimous decision. The jury is excused."

Abbie watched as the 12 men and women filed out of the courtroom and felt nauseous again knowing that they held her life in their hands. She wondered how long it would take them to decide her fate. She tried to look as innocent as she could but could feel her face scrunch up inadvertently as she swallowed the bile that rose past her gag reflex. Adding to her sweats, flashes and anxiety, she had been suffering from acid reflux too and nothing she ate would settle in her stomach. The food she had been eating in the jail didn't help and they weren't interested in getting her any homemade chicken soup to soothe her. She had been eating the fruit flavored Tums that Ben had brought her like candy. *The added calcium would at least be of some health benefit if nothing else*, she thought wryly.

"Court adjourned until further notice," Judge Rayburn tapped her gavel. The courtroom was quiet as she stood up and left. Obviously, the spectators wanted to be allowed back when the verdict was being read. They were being on their collective best behavior. As soon as she had disappeared into her chambers an excited banter burst forth in the gallery behind Abbie. It was like the judge had removed her thumb from the dyke.

"So, now what happens?" Winston leaned over the rail to give her a hug. She had almost forgotten they were there. She hugged him back and then caught site of Rachel sitting right behind them. She smiled and waved. Abbie was relieved to see her.

"I don't really know . . . Ben?"

"We wait. Hopefully not too long. I think the judge is on our side," Ben speculated. "Did you hear her? She actually reminded the jury that they would have to make damn good and sure there was no reasonable doubt if they were even to consider coming back with a guilty verdict."

"I thought that was a good sign too," Conrad chimed in. He squeezed Abbie's shoulder. "How are you holding up?"

"I could use some chicken soup," Abbie said weakly.

"We gotta go Ms. Slocum." Her young escort reached for her arm.

"We'll stop at Boston Market and pick some up," Trevor called to her. It was his favorite take-out so he'd be happy with that too but it was still sweet of him to think of it.

"That would be perfect, thanks Sweetie."

"We'll meet you back at the jail hon," Conrad blew her a kiss.

"I'll check in with you tomorrow, Abbie. Looks like you'll be in good company tonight and there's nothing more we can do at this point," Ben said walking alongside of her as she was led out the side door. "Hang in there. It's almost over."

As THEY SAT EATING their quarter chickens with sweet potatoes and gravy and a healthy dollop of mac 'n cheese, the boys grilled Abbie on what it was like to be 'on trial.'

"I bet no one else in my freshman class will have a mom who's beaten a murder rap," Winston teased as he wiped his greasy fingers on his plaid board shorts.

"I haven't beaten it yet . . . and use a napkin please," Abbie handed him a napkin and absentmindedly swirled her soup around in its bowl waiting for it to cool down. "You really should be wearing long pants. It's getting cooler at night."

"Ah, I was so hot and sweaty after wearing that darn wool suit all day I had to change." He took a long swig of his soda.

It was amazing to her how they so casually fell into their normal roles, even sitting, as she was, behind bars.

"Was that woman on the other side like that the whole time?" Trevor asked.

"You mean the prosecutor?"

"Hmmm . . ." Trevor nodded, while he chewed.

"What do you mean?"

"She was pretty scary. Definitely has a poker up her ass."

"Trevor, watch your language."

"Well, she does," Trevor reached for the barbecue sauce. "I didn't like her one little bit and I only just saw her for real today. She's been interviewed on the news and she was nasty then too."

"I didn't like her either," Winston agreed. "And, I don't think the jury liked her much. Your guy definitely had his shit together more."

"Winston, language," Abbie rolled her eyes at Conrad who shrugged. "And, my attorney's name is Ben."

"Whatever," Winston said pointing at Abbie's roll. "You gonna eat that?"

"Winston, your mother needs that more than you do," Conrad shot him a look.

"It's okay. Sure, you can have it," Abbie tossed him the roll and pushed her soup aside. "I guess I'm not very hungry after all."

"You gotta eat Abs," Conrad pushed the soup bowl back towards her. "We're not leaving until it's gone."

"Yeah. How can you have any pudding if you don't eat your meat?" The boys joined in singsong unison, quoting one of their favorite song lyrics from Pink Floyd and seeming to enjoy the role-reversal. Abbie was so relieved they were taking it so well. They were trying so hard to keep her spirits up.

"Well, okay. But, I don't want you to leave anyways. I'm so glad you're here. This waiting is awful and it's only been a few hours. I wonder how long it's going to take?"

"I really don't know," said Conrad. "It varies pretty

dramatically from case to case. And, honestly, I couldn't get a feel from this jury. I guess I'm too close to it."

"I know. They seem to have swung like a pendulum from one day to the next, although I can't really judge it very well the way my emotions have been swinging all over the place lately."

Unfortunately the swing of Abbie's moods wasn't like sitting in one of those gentle swings in a back garden and slowly swinging back and forth as you whistle a happy tune pumping your legs backwards and forward. No, Abbie couldn't help but picture one of those horrifying, thickly treaded, tire swings hung by a rope from a gnarly tree in the woods, that's tied at an unsettling angle, that spins in several directions, switching without warning as you hang on for dear life and always, unavoidably, getting your hands wrapped in, practically cutting off the circulation and almost your entire hand while screaming until someone comes to rescue you. *Wow... that was obviously a repressed childhood memory.* Abbie promised herself that after this was all over, she would definitely get some help. Her imagination was definitely running away from her as this childhood trauma came flooding back.

"Abbie, you okay? You look like you're miles away," Conrad smoothed her hair back off her forehead.

"I'm fine. Just tired I guess."

"We should go. The boys both have to work tomorrow so it'll be up and at 'em early, right guys?"

"Dad, I'm not going to work. What if the jury comes back?" Trevor hiked up his pants and started putting the empty plates in the paper bags and slurped noisily as he finished the last of his coke. He shook the ice that was left on the bottom.

"Yeah, me neither. We both want to be here for Mom," Winston put his arm around her shoulder.

"Sweetie, we don't know when that will be," Abbie took

his other hand. "And, your life has already been disrupted enough. It's amazing to me that you got through your last exams and even graduation as well as you did... thank God!"

"Guys, I'll make you a deal. You both go to work in the morning and, if there's any word, I promise, I'll come and get you," Conrad stuffed a handful of used napkins into the bag Trevor was holding.

"I guess that'll be okay. But it better be before rush week. 'Cause if it isn't, I'm not going."

"Of course you are. You can't miss that. And, besides, it's got to happen before that, doesn't it?" Abbie looked at Conrad.

"God yes. Now, let's go guys. Abbie, I'll see you tomorrow."

"Okay . . . love you guys."

Her whole gang filed out of her cell as the guard held the door open. She bit her tongue before she reminded Trevor that he needed a haircut. She hated that she couldn't see his eyes properly but figured it was pretty minor considering.

"Seems you have another visitor Ms. Slocum," the guard tilted his head towards the outer door. "You sure are a popular lady tonight."

"Oh? This late? Who?"

"Hey, look Mom, it's Rachel," Trevor waved down the corridor to her.

"Hi guys. I hope you're not leaving on my account," Rachel gave each of them a hug and kiss on both cheeks.

"No, we've got to get home. She's all yours." Conrad stepped aside so Rachel could enter the cell.

"Nice to see you boys. I'll pop by the house soon, okay? I've got some 'dorm-warming' gifts I want to get to you before you leave for school."

"Okay, catch you later Rachel," Winston was the last out and Rachel brushed her hand over his shoulder. Abbie watched them all strut down the corridor and marveled at how her boys were identical in looks but Trevor was a lot more sensitive than he let on sometimes.

"I have a real soft spot for Winston you know," Rachel put her arm around Abbie's shoulder. "I am his godmother, but I love both of your boys as much as if they were my own. You should be so proud them. Conrad too. They've been real solid through this whole mess."

The guard closed Rachel into the cell as they both plopped down on Abbie's cot.

"I'm so sorry," Abbie began but couldn't finish as silent tears filled her eyes and coursed down her cheeks.

Rachel put both her arms around her and held her until Abbie's shoulders stopped shaking and her breathing evened out. They hadn't had a chance to really talk about Joan since the trial started and Abbie didn't know where to start. Everything came rushing back on her and a fresh flood of tears started again. Abbie thought she had been all cried out.

"Sorry for what?"

"For everything! I know Joan meant a lot to you and now she's gone. I'm just sick about it."

"It wasn't your fault," Rachel soothed. "I knew Jami had a mean streak. I warned Joan that she was playing with fire even dating her."

"Really?"

"Absolutely. I knew she was in trouble when Jami copied her tattoo."

"They didn't get them together?"

"No, Joan's was designed by a friend in Key West. She went there just after she left Mark to 'find herself' and met this tattoo artist. I think she was planning to go back and live with her."

"Has anyone notified this woman?"

"I would have but I don't even know her name . . . Joan

just referred to her as 'my gorgeous tattoo artist' whenever she talked about her. She was definitely smitten. Besides, she loved the tropical weather and said she couldn't wait to get away from the cold winters here."

"Rachel, can you ever forgive me?"

"Forgive you for what? Having a good time? Being in the wrong place at the wrong time?"

"If it weren't for me, Joan would still be alive."

"You don't know that for sure. She was on a downward spiral. It was obvious that she was in a real self-destructive mode. She put on a brave face at our meetings but she told me stuff that would make your hair curl. You don't know the half of it. I'm sorry you got dragged into it Abbie. Can you forgive me?"

"For what?"

"I shouldn't have left you behind. I broke our number one cardinal rule from college. Oh God . . . I hope Conrad will forgive me too."

"Don't be ridiculous. There's nothing to forgive. We hadn't been out like that in years... you were rusty," Abbie fanned herself with the Good Housekeeping magazine the boys brought her as she felt a flush coming on. "And, Conrad's been a real rock and so supportive. He said he knows that I've been going through a tough time and he understands. The only thing he was upset about was that I took off. He made me promise I wouldn't do that again and I would always come to him if I were ever in a jam, like I always have. He said, if I can't count on him, who can I count on? Other than you, of course.

"You know that's true!" Rachel nudged her.

"I know and I'm so lucky and relieved. He's such an amazing man. I know according to the Mars and Venus thing we're supposed to be mad when our men just want to fix everything but he says we're a team and that he counts on me just as much. So, as far as Conrad is concerned, I'm in the clear."

"That's fantastic," Rachel picked up her purse. "Let's just hope the jury feels the same way. I've got to get going this was just a quick visit to see how you were holding up. But I'll check back in with you tomorrow. Fingers crossed we get a verdict soon."

Rachel motioned for the guard to let her out. "Oh, here, I brought you something to replace that magazine." She reached into her bag and tossed a mini, battery operated fan to Abbie. "They tried to take it away from me when I came in but I convinced them you couldn't possibly use the floppy rubber fan blades to harm yourself, or anyone else for that matter."

Abbie caught it and laughed. "Get outta here!"

CHAPTER 18

The fruit and yogurt with the fresh croissant and cream cheese the guard brought her in the morning was a far cry from the runny eggs and Spam that was regular breakfast fare in the jailhouse. Abbie wondered if Conrad had anything to do with it. She hadn't complained but she supposed the untouched plate day after day probably spoke volumes. She actually enjoyed her breakfast for the first time in weeks. She wasn't expecting Conrad until the afternoon and Ben said he would see her as soon as he heard anything, so she was on her own. What would she do to keep herself busy?

She glanced down at the stack of magazines the boys had brought and thought that would be a good start. She had always been busy and was the type who had a jam-packed calendar... with two active boys who were into every sport and after school activity imaginable, it wasn't very difficult. The last several weeks had also gone by in a blur and this was the first time she had nothing imminent to get ready for. The day stretched out in front of her like a long ink-black tunnel with a tiny pinprick of light way off in the distance. Behind that pinprick of light she imagined a jury of 12 of her peers, who were deliberating on her very life and would be deciding how the next 10 years would pan out. Abbie shook herself and tried not to think about it. Worrying about it wasn't going to help one way or another and would just put lots of negative energy into the air which she didn't want wafting into the atmosphere and somehow landing in the very room the jurors were sequestered. *I'll just think of this as some well-deserved 'me time,' I don't get that very often.*

She cracked open the *Good Housekeeping*, recognizing the irony as she looked at her surroundings. She wondered what Martha Stewart did when she was in same situation? What were the boys thinking when they brought her this? As she was flipping through, Abbie noticed a page turned down at the corner. She felt a huge smile take over her face. The boys had left her a not so subtle message. There in full-color was a picture of a gorgeously rich, mouthwatering blueberry grunt, oozing with the indigo blue syrupy sauce that comes from cooking the berries. The liquefied berries swirled through the puffed up tea biscuit dough. It was enough to make Abbie's stomach growl with anticipation. A step-by-step recipe sat in a separate box off to the side of the page. It was almost blueberry season and they always went picking blueberries as a family and Abbie always made blueberry jam, blueberry pies and blueberry grunt. She made a mental note that the first thing she would do when she got out would be to put this recipe to good use.

She rifled through the pile and saw that they had also brought her a *People Magazine*. Now that was more like it. She had stacks of them in her bathroom and they knew it was her favorite . . . one of the only magazines she always read cover to cover, and even did the crossword puzzle every time. She flipped to the 'make-over' section, which she always went to first, and there was a sticky note in Conrad's handwriting: "We owe you one day at the spa. Redeemable as soon as you're free!

Love, Conrad, Winston and Trevor." *Jeez, they did pay attention.*

Abbie was staring at the sticky note and crying when Ben arrived.

"Abbie, what's the matter?" Ben asked as the guard closed the cell door behind him. He hung his suit jacket on the metal chair.

Abbie handed him the magazine, too choked up to answer. Ben read the note and laughed.

"So, why are you crying? Looks like you've got something to look forward to."

"I know," Abbie sobs started anew. "I just don't deserve them."

"Don't be so foolish, of course you do. Now, get a grip, wipe your nose and pay attention," Ben tried to sound stern but Abbie knew better. He handed her a *Boston Market* napkin that was left on the table from the night before. "The jury has come back with their decision and we've got to be in court in less than two hours."

"Oh my God . . . so soon?" Abbie wiped her eyes and blew her nose into the napkin.

"Yes and I think it's a good sign. I've called Conrad and he's on his way over with a fresh outfit for you. He'll drop it off so you can get ready and then he's going to go pick up your sons and meet us back at the courthouse. Abbie, this is it."

"Jesus, I think I'm going to puke," Abbie could feel the anxiety rising from her gut, like icy little fingers creeping into her lungs and wrapping around her esophagus. She shivered. "It feels like someone's just walked over my grave." Abbie cringed.

"Come on Abbie, you've been doing great. Don't fall apart on me now." Ben sat down beside her and put his hand on her shoulder. "Breathe deeply. That's it . . . inhale, exhale. You're okay."

"What's up Ben? Is she okay?" Conrad thanked the guard for letting him in and turned to Abbie with a grave look.

"I'm fine, I'm fine," Abbie managed. "The news just caught me a little by surprise. I didn't think it would come so soon. Conrad, I'm scared." Abbie was rocking back and forth on the cot with her arms crossed tightly in front of her.

Ben got up and Conrad took the spot next to Abbie he had vacated and gathered her in his arms. "Abbie, whatever the outcome is, we'll deal with it. We're all here for you—me, Ben, Rachel, the boys." He took her face in his hands and looked deep into her eyes. "We always will be."

Abbie took a deep, shuddering breath. "You can't imagine how much that means to me."

"I know." Conrad kissed her forehead. "You going to be okay? You've got to get ready." He handed her a garment bag. "Everything you need should be in there. I got you a new suit. It's a deep purple. Rachel helped me pick it out. We thought the occasion called for a little more color than the blacks and browns you've been wearing. I hope you don't mind."

"No, it sounds lovely," Abbie replied.

"You got shoes and a shirt in there and I even put a pair of earrings in the jacket pocket. Actually, I have to admit, that was Winston's idea. I threw some make-up in too. I hope it's the right stuff. Do you need any help?"

"No, I'll be fine. You just go get the boys," Abbie reached up and put her hand on his face. Conrad covered her tiny hand with his own, which totally enveloped it. He pulled it away from his face and kissed her palm. He turned to Ben.

"Okay. I'll see you both there."

"Rock 'n roll," Ben shook Conrad's hand. "I'll follow you out."

As both men departed Abbie stood gripping the edges of the garment bag Conrad had given her and prayed, more fervently than she had throughout this whole ordeal. She desperately hoped He was listening.

———

ABBIE CLOSED HER EYES, leaned her head on the back seat of the police cruiser en route to the courthouse and tried to calm her nerves. Her mind was going a hundred miles a minute. She felt like there was a vortex of voices in her head all telling her to chill out, relax, take a pill, hang in there and not to worry; all overlapping simultaneously with the doomsayers chanting you're going to jail, you're a horrible person and how could you do it?

The panicky feeling she'd had earlier had relinquished its hold on her throat but it still hovered in the pit of her stomach, threatening to erupt at any minute. She continued to breathe deeply and tried to concentrate on the cheerleaders in her head instead of the hecklers. *Today's the day I'm going home.* Abbie nodded her head firmly and noticed the cop in the front seat watching her in the rearview mirror and wondered if she'd been talking out loud.

"Just giving myself a pep-talk," she said in way of explanation.

"We're all rooting for you down at the station, Mrs. Slocum," he offered as he pulled up behind the courthouse and parked.

"Thanks. I need all the positive energy I can get," she smiled at him as he helped her out of the car. No matter how much they were 'rooting for her' Abbie was still cuffed. So much for 'innocent until proven guilty.' If that were the case, she would have been home over the past... what was it? Six weeks? *Shit, that's a long time to be locked up. I just hope I spent my last night as a jailbird.* She looked up at a beautiful, crystal blue sky and said another little prayer. She hadn't prayed so much since she was little and said her bedtime prayers with her mother every night. She hoped that wasn't a strike against her with The Man upstairs.

It was still a half hour before the jury was set to come back so Abbie was led into one of the conference rooms where Ben, Conrad, Rachel and the boys were already waiting. There they sat... her real, live cheering section.

"You guys all look like you're going to a wedding," Abbie tugged on Winston's tie.

"We're taking you out to celebrate as soon as we're done here," Trevor stepped forward and hugged her.

"Ever the optimist. I hope that doesn't jinx it." Abbie picked some non-existent lint off his shoulder. "You all look very handsome. And, you got your hair cut!"

"Yeah . . . it's your 'release day' present." Trevor grinned.

"Hey Sweetie," Rachel took her hand and squeezed. "We're going to be right behind you."

"Okay you guys. Now that you've seen our star, better go and get some good seats. We'll be called in shortly." Ben ushered them all out and closed the door behind them.

"You ready?" He turned to Abbie.

"Ready as I'll ever be. And, Ben?"

"Yeah?"

"Thanks for everything. You've been amazing through all this."

"You're welcome Abbie. But, I'm just doing my job." He winked at her. But Abbie knew it was more than that. She and Conrad had developed a strong friendship with Ben throughout the trial. He and his team had been not only efficient and professional, but also warm and sympathetic and genuinely concerned for her wellbeing. It had kept her going through some of the toughest days. She also knew that he had charged them a fraction of what he normally did. Abbie didn't question why and was hugely grateful to him.

"Ben, I have to ask you something," Abbie began tentatively. Even though she felt they had become close through the trial, she didn't know where the professional relationship stopped and how much of his personal life he was willing to share.

"Sure, shoot."

"I couldn't help noticing when we first met and shook hands that you had callouses on yours," Abbie looked down at his hands.

"Yeah, I guess I do," Ben turned both his hands up and looked at his palms.

"Well, as a guy who goes to an office in a shirt and tie every day, I thought that was a little strange. It's not like you're a farm worker or something." Abbie's grandfather had owned a farm and she remembered his big, gentle hands quite fondly. "How did they get so calloused?"

"Well, I like to chop wood," Ben said quite matter-of-factly. "And, I like to carve."

"Really?"

"Yes, I find the chopping helps me release some of the stress of the job and the carving is something that allows me to use a little of my creative side."

"You have a creative side?" Abbie knew there was much more to Ben than met the eye and she hoped she and Conrad would have a chance to meet Ben's family after the trial was over.

"Yeah, my mom was an artist and I think I got a little of her creative gene in me."

"We have a lot more in common then... my mom was an artist too. But, how much wood do you need? Surely you don't chop enough to do that," Abbie motioned towards his hands.

"Well, my wife and I decided to get a wood stove to help support my habit," Ben laughed. "It really does help relieve the stress and it's great exercise. We love a nice warm fire in the middle of winter too. We pretty much heat the whole house with it. Saves a ton on our electric bill."

"You're full of surprises," Abbie mused. He was a rich, criminal lawyer who cut his own firewood and used a wood stove to save money on his electric bill. *Go figure.*

"Mr. Hurst, they're ready for you," the clerk popped his head in the conference room.

"Okay, thanks. We'll be right there." He turned to Abbie. "Let's get in there and see what wonderful things your future holds."

"From your lips to God's ears," Abbie said hopefully.

CHAPTER 19

The courtroom was buzzing with excitement as Abbie entered with Ben and made her way to the defendant's table. She hoped it would be for the last time. This room and the whole building were looking way too familiar to her. She knew every crack and crevice; every thread on the chairs at the defendant's table; all the swirls in the grain of the wood on the table and every water stain on the ceiling of the old courtroom.

She heard her name called several times when she had walked up the courthouse steps. She was almost mobbed and a few people even reached out to touch her like she was some sort of celebrity. Inside it was standing room only. She wanted to scream, *Don't you people have lives?* But, it was human nature to want to see inside the deepest, darkest recesses of the lives of other people, especially when there was a sordid twist to it. It was what had triggered the proliferation of reality shows on television. It was the same thing when there was a traffic accident. She was the carnage strewn all over the road and these people were the rubberneckers who just couldn't help themselves, gawking at another's misfortunes, some even taking pictures.

She scanned the crowd as she walked through but only recognized one face. *Holy shit! It's Bess.* There in the middle of the melee was Abbie's neighbor, soaking it all in. She really shouldn't have been surprised. Bess probably felt it was her duty as the neighborhood gossip to be on hand to fill in anyone who actually had a job to go to. The rest were total strangers. It felt like a soap opera when there were crazy fans who developed an attachment to a character. They believed that since they watched the show every day they knew the person who was playing the role personally and it gave them the right to get involved in their business. Abbie tried to smile because it seemed like the general feeling in the room was supportive for the most part but it still made her a little uneasy. She figured there was probably a contingent that also wanted to see her convicted, just for the drama of it. Finally, her gaze landed on the familiar faces she wanted to see. Conrad, Trevor, Winston and Rachel were in the first row right behind the railing. They all gave her the double thumbs up sign as she took her seat.

Ben squeezed her hand and nodded at Abbie's cheering section that had taken over the front row. They watched the jury file in. Abbie noted that they seemed a little lighter in their collective step than before. She hoped that was a good sign. The jury forewoman even smiled in her direction. Abbie's heart skipped a beat.

"All rise, the Honorable Judge Courtney Rayburn presiding." The bailiff delivered his line in a monotone developed after years of uttering the same phrase over and over again, day after day, trial after trial.

"Please be seated," Judge Rayburn sat down and organized the paperwork in front of her, scanned the courtroom and inclined her head towards Abbie, then turned to the Jury. "Have you reached a verdict?"

The foreman stood up and faced the judge. "We have Your

Honor." She handed a folded piece of paper that had either one, or two all-important words written on it that would dictate the next phase of Abbie's life. Abbie couldn't breathe. It felt like all the air in the room had been sucked out along with the motion of the bailiff's hand that took the note from the foreman and swept across the courtroom and handed it to the Judge.

Judge Rayburn unfolded the paper in what seemed to Abbie to be in horribly painful slow motion.

"Abbie, breathe," Ben leaned over and whispered in her ear.

Abbie let go of the breath she was holding and felt light-headed.

"Will the defendant please rise?" Judge Rayburn nodded at Abbie and waited for her to get to her feet. Ben took a hold of her elbow and she leaned into him gratefully.

"What say you?" The Judge took off her glasses, holding up the paper she still had in her hand.

"We the jury, find the defendant, Abigail Slocum, not guilty of the offense of murder in the second degree." The forewoman seemed to be letting go of the weight of the world sitting squarely on her shoulders as she read the words off her copy of the jury verdict form.

A squeal came from behind and Abbie was sure it was Rachel. Abbie hugged Ben and turned and smiled at her entourage. Ben reached over and shook Conrad and Rachel's hands and gave Winston and Trevor a high five. The court-room erupted into lively discussion.

"Please, ladies and gentlemen, order!" Judge Rayburn banged her gavel and waited for the din to calm down. "Thank you madam foreman and thank you ladies and gentlemen of the jury for your time and service." Judge Rayburn acknowl-edged the 12 jurists. "Now that the trial is over, may I remind you that as jurors you are under no obligation to answer any questions about the case or comment upon it in any way. However, if you do wish to speak with the media or attorneys about the trial, you may do so but you are not permitted, under any circumstances, to reveal the substance of the discussions among members of the jury. The jury is dismissed."

The judge then turned her attention to Abbie, who had finally let out her breath, tears of relief streaming down her face. Ben was holding her arm as Abbie's knees had almost buckled from underneath her.

"Ms. Slocum, you are free to go, but I would like to make a suggestion."

"Yes Your Honor?"

"During this trial, you have admitted to having serious mood swings, bouts of depression and thoughts of suicide," Judge Rayburn paused.

Abbie nodded slowly but couldn't say anything because of the huge lump that had re-formed in her throat. If she didn't know better she would have thought that the courtroom was empty because you could have heard a pin drop.

"Ms. Slocum . . . Abbie . . . I would strongly recommend that you seek the help of a medical professional. I'm sure this case hasn't helped with your anxiety and it's probably made your other symptoms worse as well. It looks like you have a very strong support network and you need to take advantage of that but they aren't medical professionals and you shouldn't try to handle this alone. Please take care of yourself and your family."

"Yes ma'am," Abbie managed to get out.

Judge Rayburn smiled. "Court Adjourned."

Conrad came through the gate and wrapped Abbie in a bear hug. The boys hung back. Abbie realized that they still had a lot to absorb. As mature and understanding and supportive as they were, the whole issue of menopause was pretty foreign to them and it was probably more than a little scary to see their mother falling apart in front of their eyes.

Abbie extricated herself from Conrad's arms. "Come here boys," she reached for her sons and was quickly enveloped. Abbie was 5' 7" but cocooned in the arms of two strapping guys, who were more than 6' 3", she looked like a shrimp. She had pretty much disappeared.

"I have to say, this is the best medicine I could ever hope for," Abbie sighed. "Okay guys, you've heard stuff that I'm sure has you a bit concerned. I promise you that I am going to take care of myself and you don't have to worry one bit about me doing anything crazy."

"You mean like the tattoo," Winston winked at her.

"What tattoo?" Conrad asked.

"You guys can talk about that later," Rachel broke in. "We have some celebrating to do."

Conrad looked quizzically at Abbie. She shrugged, tilted her head and lifted her hair so he could see the little pink rose nestled behind her ear. He leaned down to have a closer look and Abbie held her breath as she could feel his on her neck.

"Well, well, well," Conrad chuckled. "That's actually pretty sexy." He leaned in and kissed Abbie's neck. She tingled from head to toe, sighed and put her head on his chest. Conrad wrapped his arm tightly around her shoulder and squeezed. Abbie linked her arm through Rachel's as they exited the courthouse together.

"I think I'm going to hurl," Abbie heard Trevor comment, following closely behind.

"Don't be such a jerk," Winston admonished.

Abbie sighed again and smiled to herself. Things were getting back to normal already. Then she felt the all-too familiar sensation as her body became infused with heat . . . *Well, almost.*

ACKNOWLEDGMENTS

There are so many people who have helped along the way but I must start with my biggest fan who was always my first beta reader.

Thank you Mother Theresa, MT for short (my real mother), whose name is Theresa and, after raising five kids, she should be sainted! She's not only my mother, but also my best friend and my therapist (I've lost count of the number of hours sitting at the kitchen table pouring out my soul to her always listening and sympathetic, non-judgemental ears, usually followed by some sage advice or a funny comment that would send us into peels of laughter). She doesn't remember actually experiencing any serious menopause symptoms but she *was* a widow at the time with three teenagers still at home so didn't have time for such 'foolishness'. She was the first reader of *Mental Pause* and she loved it! She wanted to know who Joan was!

I realize that your mom is supposed to love everything you do so I took a deep breath and shared it with my next ~~victim~~, err ~~guinea pig~~, err test reader... My mother-in-law, Ruth. She and I have shared books back and forth for more than 22 years and she always has such thoughtful insight (I've read the most obscure books on her recommendations, helping broaden my literary horizons). One day as I was telling her about the plot line for a novel I was thinking about writing, she told me her own tale of peri-menopausal woes, which happened to kick-in while she was teaching high school French to some very rowdy boys. The exciting thing about Ruth being one of my first readers is that it turns out that the launch day I chose for *Mental Pause*, March 8, 2013 (International Women's Day) is also her birthday. So, Happy Birthday Ruth!

It continued on from there as I got braver and braver, widening the circles of those avid readers who were in my target audience from whom I asked for honest feedback. Thank you my trusted family members (sister Sue – who passed on the t-shirt with the black cat; cousin Susan, sister-in-law Violet, cousin Anne and Aunt Noni); close girlfriends (Michele – a most amazing proof-reader and editor; Katie – who is part of my writing group, Flamingo Authors; and Barb – a lifelong friend who is working on her first novel!); writer friends and colleagues (Zvezdana – author of Dubai Wives; Linda – blogger at Adventures in Expatland and co-author of Turning Points; and Vebeke – part of Flamingo Authors); my publisher for @Home in Dubai, Jo Parfitt from Summertime Publishing and Stacey Donovan, author, editor and author mentor. Without all your enthusiastic encouragement I wouldn't have launched on this journey. My heartfelt thanks go out to you all! I hope you're all ready for the next one!

Note: With this re-released edition, I kept my acknowledgements as is but will note that my mom passed away in 2024 at the age of ninety-nine. We were blessed to have her for so long!

ABOUT THE AUTHOR

Anne Louise O'Connell grew up in Halifax, Nova Scotia and has lived around the world, escaping the cold of Canada on a hunt for warmer climes, with stops in Florida, Dubai, and Thailand. In 2007, after seventeen years in the PR business, she decided to focus on her real passion and just write. In 2016, she returned to her hometown and established OC Publishing.

In addition to being a partner/hybrid publisher, O'Connell is a multi-genre author who has written both fiction and non-fiction. Her first novel, *Mental Pause*, won an Independent Publisher Magazine (IPPY) Bronze Book Award, and her second novel, *Deep Deceit*, is the first in the Deep Mysteries series. Book II, *Deep Freeze*, came out in March 2025. The third in the series, *Deep River*, will release in 2027. She has also published a collection of her expat living and travel stories titled *Swimming with the Elephants and Other Adventures*.

While living in Thailand, she was a contributing writer for The Wall Street Journal Expat Blog and Global Living Magazine and a regular columnist for Expat Focus. O'Connell is a two-time graduate of Mount St. Vincent University: Early

Childhood Education (1984), hence her love of children's literature; and a Bachelor of Public Relations (1990).

Connect with Anne:

Website: www.ocpublishing.ca
YouTube channel: www.youtube.com/OCPublishing
Facebook: www.facebook.com/ocpublishing
LinkedIn: www.linkedin.com/in/annelouiseoconnell
Instagram: @ocpubhfx
TikTok: @ocpubhfx

ALSO BY
ANNE LOUISE O'CONNELL

Deep Deceit (Deep Mysteries Book I)

Deep Freeze (Deep Mysteries Book II)

Swimming with the Elephants and Other Adventures